"LADIES A........ . .
HOLLY AND THE HEAR...... ...ERS!"

The kid, riding the tiger, grabs the microphone, pumping it up, taking it higher, making it hotter, rounding the bend and racing for home.

> *They say I'm bad,*
> *But you know better.*

Arranging her hair with a shake of her head, so that it falls about her shoulders, the kid spins around, spreads her legs wide, props her fists on her hips, beams a knowing smile, and sings—

> *And baby, baby, baby,*
> *I'm your heart's desire.*

The spotlight snaps off.

The stage is black.

The crowd sits a moment, as if they were stunned and catching their breath. And then they go totally wild!

Other Avon Flare Books by
Bruce and Carole Hart

BREAKING UP IS HARD TO DO
CROSS YOUR HEART
NOW OR NEVER
SOONER OR LATER
WAITING GAMES

Avon Books are available at special quantity discounts for bulk purchases for sales promotions, premiums, fund raising or educational use. Special books, or book excerpts, can also be created to fit specific needs.

For details write or telephone the office of the Director of Special Markets, Avon Books, Dept. FP, 1350 Avenue of the Americas, New York, New York 10019, 1-800-238-0658.

STRUT

BRUCE and CAROLE HART

AN AVON FLARE BOOK

STRUT is an original publication of Avon Books. This work has never before appeared in book form. This work is a novel. Any similarity to actual persons or events is purely coincidental.

AVON BOOKS
A division of
The Hearst Corporation
1350 Avenue of the Americas
New York, New York 10019

Copyright © 1992 by The Laughing Willow Company, Inc.
Published by arrangement with The Laughing Willow Company, Inc.
Library of Congress Catalog Card Number: 91-92460
ISBN: 0-380-75962-4
RL: 4.8

First Avon Flare Printing: June 1992

AVON FLARE TRADEMARK REG. U.S. PAT. OFF. AND IN OTHER COUNTRIES, MARCA REGISTRADA, HECHO EN U.S.A.

Printed in the U.S.A.

RA 10 9 8 7 6 5 4 3 2 1

I don't know how to tell this to you so you'll believe it, but it's true—I swear to God!—all of it, including the part about the ghost . . .

ONE

There's a bonfire blazing on the beach across the road from the Cobblestone Inn in Wildwood on the New Jersey shore, and the night breeze blowing in off the ocean stirs its flames and it sets them swirling like the skirts of a gypsy girl dancing barefoot over the sand and it showers the air with sparks like moonlight shimmering on her golden earrings, as she tosses back her head and laughs aloud at the vast and fathomless sky. . . .

"Want to dance?"

I turn from the window in the bar at the Cobblestone, and standing in front of me I see Jim Sweeney, home from college, looking tall, dark, and snobby as ever, and I'm amazed.

I mean, up until now, Jim Sweeney has never even spoken to me. Up until now, it's like he didn't even know that I existed.

And now, I suppose, just because his sister Barbara is going to marry my brother Bryan in a couple of weeks, here he is, finally noticing that I'm alive and asking me to—

"No, thanks," says Claudia.

Whoops! For a second there, I almost forgot that I was invisible—which I am most of the time, but which I am most especially when I'm out with my best friend, Claudia Jones, who is so great looking even really pretty girls seem to disappear into thin air when she's around.

Thanks to her mother, the fair-skinned, Cuban-born

1

Estelle, and her father, Israel, a black Venezuelan from Marácaibo, Claudia's got a perfect cocoa-butter complexion, coal-black eyes, black curly hair, perky little boobs, and long, long legs that her boyfriend, Eddie, told her, the first time he laid eyes on her, set his mind to "dreaming up knots like they don't teach you in the Boy Scouts."

I mean—

> She's a one punch knock-out,
> A real teen queen.
> A walking dream,
> If you know what I mean!
> Bop! Bop!

"*Not bad!*" I tell myself, awarding me a 9.2 for my latest attempt at capturing Claudia in an unsung song.

"Oh, come on," Jim Sweeney pleads with Claudia.

"I'm with somebody," Claudia tells him.

Jim Sweeney looks at me and says, "I'm sure Holly won't mind."

I give him a look.

Claudia laughs. "I'm with Eddie Ballard," she says. "He's the drummer with Bent. We're here to root for them, so—"

"*You* are!" I remind her. "I don't root for bands that won't let my best friend play with them just because she's a girl."

"So they can win the Playoff tonight," she continues.

"Without you," I point out to her.

"And go on to the Showdown," she explains.

"And compete for the five thousand dollar prize," I add.

"And the chance," she continues, "that somebody from some record company will see them and offer them a contract."

"Like they did with Joey Doyle and Night Train," I

2

add, for Jim Sweeney's information. "I don't suppose you heard about that over on Shore Road."

Which is a dig, of course, because he must have, since by now practically everybody in the world knows the story of how, back five or six years ago, Joey Doyle got discovered playing on an Amateur Night here at the Cobblestone and how, according to *Rolling Stone,* he went on from there to become "the biggest baddest rock star to come swaggering onto the scene since 'Demon Jim' Morrison first started lighting fires and burning bridges over twenty long years ago"—which just happens to be the true-life, rags-to-riches story that put the Playoffs and the Showdown and the Cobblestone Inn and Wildwood, New Jersey, on the map.

"Word reached us," says Jim Sweeney.

"Let's hear it for Leslie Lee and the Leroys!" shouts Arthur Kilburn, as he bounds onto the stage where the house band has been treating the overflow crowd to an industrial-strength medley of "Hits from the Sixties."

The Cobblestone's owner and the man who runs the shows, Arthur leads the crowd in a quick round of applause and then, as Leslie and the Leroys file off the stage, he turns back to the audience and shouts, "It's Monday night—Amateur Night! And for the fifth year running, it's time to kick off the Cobblestone's world famous Amateur Night Playoffs!"

As the crowd applauds and cheers, Jim Sweeney looks over at Claudia and shrugs and, like there was ever a chance that she'd dance with him, he tells her, "It's too late, anyway."

"The day you were born," I tell him, as the applause builds and the cheering mounts and—from somewhere too close behind me—some dick lets loose with a single, ear-piercing, fingers-in-the-mouth-type whistle, which is so loud in my ears I wince and whip around, ready to strangle the—

Wonderful! Standing just inside the front door and look-

3

ing over the bar and down into the show room, his arms folded across his chest, his eyes searching the crowd, I spot a cop.

Have I mentioned my age? Seventeen?

And this cop that I spot isn't just any old cop, either.

"So, if everybody's ready . . ." shouts Arthur Kilburn.

"Ready!" the crowd roars.

No, this cop that I spot just happens to be the chief of the Wildwood Police Department and everybody's first choice for the biggest dick of all, Chief Roland Hanna—My *father! Pop!*—who has threatened to kill me if he ever catches me here.

"Okay, then," shouts Arthur, "let's everybody put your hands together, and let's have a big Cobblestone welcome for Bent!"

As the crowd bursts into applause, I tell Claudia, "Good night."

Following my gaze to the front door, Claudia shrinks back into the shadows as I turn and plunge into the crowd.

I'm on my way, making a beeline for the exit door at the side of the bandstand, when I hear someone behind me—I'd swear it's Jim Sweeney—laughing his ass off.

TWO

It's Sunday, June 14, and it couldn't be a prettier day. It's bright and sunny, hot but—with the breeze off the ocean—not too hot.

And the house, the Sweeneys' house—if you happen to like beautiful old country houses that are set back from winding roads on graded lawns overlooking sandy beaches and glittering seas—it couldn't be much prettier either.

So it's a perfect day and a perfect place for my brother Bryan's wedding.

And I wish I was dead.

Because of who he's marrying—Barbara Sweeney, who is Jim Sweeney's sister and the only daughter of Jock Sweeney and his wife, Heloise, who own quite a lot of Wildwood, starting with Sweeney's Coal and Gas and who, with their rich friends, lord over everything that they don't actually own.

The first time I heard about Bryan and Barbara Sweeney was last summer, when I was working, like I am again this summer, behind the counter at Avery's, this hot dog stand on the old boardwalk down at the beach.

"Yo! Holly!"

Adele Gallant calls to me from the other side of the counter behind me.

As I turn around, ready to say, "Yo! Adele," she jerks her head toward the boardwalk and says, "Ya' seen the lovebirds?"

So I look up the boardwalk in the direction that she's jerking her head and—

Jesus! It's Bryan!

He's on a break from his job as a lifeguard, wearing just his lifeguard uniform—a sun tan, a speedsuit, and a pair of floppy sandals—and he's walking along the boardwalk holding hands with—

I can't believe my eyes!

Like she's Julia Roberts or somebody! In this huge, potato chip of a sun hat, this gauzy, off-the-shoulder sundress, and these dainty, wedge-heeled espadrilles, walking along the boardwalk and holding hands with my favorite brother, Bryan, it's—

"Barbara Sweeney?!"

It's the next morning before I catch up with Bryan. By the time he hauls himself out of bed and pulls on a pair of jeans and drags himself into the kitchen, Pop's long gone and I'm about to be.

I hit him with it, the sixty-four-million-dollar question, as soon as he stumbles through the door.

"Barbara Sweeney?!"

Squinting in the sunlight and scratching his head, he says, "Yeah. Why?"

"That's what I'd like to know!" I tell him.

He laughs and shakes his head, pads over to the coffee-pot, and pours himself a cup.

"You mean, why am I going out with her?" he asks me.

"You're going out with her?!"

"Saturday night," he says.

"She's a—*Sweeney!*" I remind him.

"I forgive her," he says.

"Well, I don't!" I tell him.

He looks at me.

"I mean, I would. I would forgive her for having everything that she could ever want—good looks and nice clothes, a fine family, money to burn—"

"Donnie Pelligrino?" he asks me, mentioning the name of this friend of his who used to go out with Barbara and who—like everybody else in town—I happened to have had a major crush on.

"Yes!" I lie. "I'd forgive her for Donnie, too."

Bryan grins like he doesn't believe me.

"But . . . ?" he says.

"I don't know," I tell him. "It isn't just that she's got everything that she could ask for. What pisses me off is the way she pretends that her having everything that she could ask for doesn't make any difference.

"And how she expects you to pretend that it doesn't make any difference, too, when you both know damned well that it makes all the difference in the world.

"I mean, the way she's got it set up, you're not even allowed to envy her without feeling like you're a bad sport or something.

6

"Which is why, every time I see her bopping down the boardwalk or see her smiling or just picture her smiling in my mind, I want to hit her with a pie because—

"Because she just ticks me off, that's all!"

Bryan grins and says, "I like her."

"Why?!" I ask him. "She can't be any fun to—"

"She is!"

"—be with," I tell him. "She can't be! Unless—"

A terrible thought crosses my kind.

"Oh, no! You're not—!"

"What?" says Bryan, grinning, like he knows what I'm thinking, but daring me to come out with it.

"You'd better be careful!" I warn him.

"Holly . . ."

"Well, you'd better!" I insist.

He smiles.

"Okay," he says, "I will."

"You will?" I ask him.

Suddenly I'm afraid that I've put the wrong idea in his head.

He nods and says, "If it comes up."

I look at him.

He looks at me.

And we both crack up.

And then, after a second, because I know it's really none of my business what Bryan does and who he does it with, I tell him, "I'm sorry."

"It's okay," he says.

"But except for Rollie and Eddie," I tell him, "you're the only brother I've got."

He laughs and "Hey," he says, "you're not getting rid of me, if that's what you're thinking. I'm just taking the girl out to the movies, you know? It's not like I'm asking her to marry me . . ."

Talk about famous last words! Beginning that weekend, Bryan sees Barbara Sweeney every weekend and nearly every weekday night all summer long.

And then, when summer's over and they go off to college—Bryan to Syracuse and Barbara Sweeney to Swarthmore—they see each other weekends and vacations until—

"Bry . . . ?"

It's Easter vacation. Bryan's back from school and dragging in after another night at the Sweeneys'. I don't know what time it is, only that I'm fast asleep when I wake up to the sound of him climbing the stairs to his room in the attic.

The minute he opens the door to my room, I know it. I can see it in his face, he's so disgustingly happy.

"Hi," he says. "Guess what?"

"You won the lottery?"

He shakes his head.

"Just as good, though," he says.

I feel a chill shoot up my back and stick me between my shoulder blades.

"Barbara Sweeney?"

Bryan nods.

"We're getting married," he says.

Even though I knew it the second that I saw him, I still can't believe it!

"To each other?" I ask him.

"Uh-huh," he says.

"No joke?"

He shakes his head.

"When?"

"June," he says.

"This June?!"

"Why wait?" he asks me.

Because, I think, *if you wait a little while, there's a chance that you might come to your senses! Because, right now, you're so crazy about Barbara Sweeney it's like you've forgotten all about yourself!*

"What about you?" I ask him.

"What about me?" he says.

"You were going to turn yourself into a writer, remember?"

"Yeah," he says.

"Well, how are you going to do that with a wife hanging around your neck? And kids? And a mortgage and all that? What are you going to write about, if that's all you know?

"And what about us? We were supposed to meet in Paris and hitchhike through Europe together and tramp around Africa and . . ."

"Hey," he says.

I can't help it. There are tears in my eyes and there's nothing I can do about it.

"Take it easy," he says. "We can still do all that."

I shake my head and tell him, "No."

"Yes," he says. "The three of us."

"No," I tell him.

"Sure," he says.

And that's when it dawns on me, the reason why Bryan *can't* wait to get married, the only logical explanation for his thinking that he's *got to* marry Barbara Sweeney.

Which is why, while Bryan goes on telling me that Barbara Sweeney is the best thing that ever happened to him, in my head I'm screaming at him, *"No! Don't do it! Just because you're a nice guy and you want to do the right thing, don't just throw your life away and chuck all your dreams!*

"Just because you knocked her up, that doesn't mean you have to go and marry the girl! You don't have to, Bryan! You mustn't! You can't!"

And then, suddenly, Pop's at the door.

Bryan's kneeling at the side of my bed by now, and I've got my head buried under my pillow and I'm sobbing my heart out, and suddenly I hear—

"Do you have any idea what hour of the morning this is, either of you, to be waking your father from a sound

9

sleep with all your shouting and carrying on? If you don't mind my asking?''

So, Bryan says he's sorry and—before Pop can tell him that he should be—he tells him the ''good news.''

And Pop, the old bastard, as soon as he hears it, he turns to mush.

''The Sweeney girl, is it?'' he says.

Good guess, Pop!

''Yes,'' Bryan tells him, ''Barbara.''

''Ah, son!'' says Pop, his eyes filling with tears, as he takes Bryan in his arms and gives him a big hug, ''Your mother, God rest her soul, your mother would be so proud!''

And I can't help it. It's like there's a knife in my gut. And like somebody's twisting it, I howl . . .

THREE

Party Hat! Party Hat!
Don't forget your Party Hat!
Party Hat! Party Hat!
If you're gonna' party!

I feel like a female impersonator. As I stand looking at myself upstairs in the Sweeney's guest room, where Barbara Sweeney's bridal attendants are getting set for the main event, I feel like one of those guys who puts on a wig and a dress and pretends that he's Marilyn Monroe.

Not that I look like Marilyn Monroe who, when I think

10

about it, was like an inflatable Madonna, all round and soft and easy.

No, Nicky Ambrose, who is Barbara Sweeney's roommate from college and her maid of honor, except for her hair, which is pitch-black and shiny as a raven's wings, *she* looks like Marilyn Monroe.

Which is probably why she's so hot to get back her spot in front of the mirror. Nicky Ambrose probably adores looking at herself.

Me, on the other hand, even when I'm wearing my own clothes, instead of this slippery, blue satin, floor-length bridesmaid's gown with dyed-to-match pumps, I don't like to spend any more time in front of mirrors than I absolutely have to.

And it isn't because I'm modest, either. No, it's more like I'm so vain, I can't stand to be reminded of how far from pretty I am.

I've got good hair, copper red, that I wear long and don't do much of anything with except wash it every now and then and get it cut when I can't stand it anymore.

And my eyes are blue like cornflowers. But my nose is just a nose. And my mouth is just a mouth. And although my complexion is clear, it's also freckled.

So, all together, my face is what you'd call a nice enough face, if you happened to notice. But it's not so nice that you would, necessarily. Notice, I mean.

My body's that way too—adequate for keeping my head from resting on the tops of my shoes, with a curve or two here or there but mostly there—back there, instead of up here.

Which adds up to about five foot six inches and one hundred and fourteen pounds of— "Adorable," says Nicky Ambrose.

"Pardon me?" I say.

"Oh, that's all right," says Nicky, gently shoving me aside and taking my spot in front of the mirror, "but take my word for it, you couldn't look any sweeter. Do you think Donnie will show up?''

She addresses this question to me while running an inventory of her own perfect features in the mirror, but she's actually talking to the bridesmaids—three pretty young women, natives of Wildwood and friends of Barbara Sweeney's from way back—who are standing across the room by the bay window with the window seat and the breathtaking view of the ocean.

Not sure if she's heard Nicky right, April Raines looks over at her and says, ''Do you mean Donnie Pelligrino?''

Donnie Pelligrino! The name alone, just hearing it, even now after all these years . . .

''I don't suppose he could, could he?'' says Nicky. ''I mean, isn't he playing ball somewhere?''

I was so in love with him. So madly in love. And just because everybody else was too that didn't make any difference to me.

''Boston,'' says Helen Caine.

''Not yet,'' says April, correcting her. ''He's still recovering from the operation.''

He was so great looking, so tall and dark and so handsome he was almost pretty, like a statue that you'd see in a museum, his shape was that classical. And his muscles were so right there, you could almost feel them with your eyes.

''Rotator cuff,'' Lenny Odoms explains.

''He's working back into shape,'' says April.

''In Boston,'' Helen insists.

Of course, being Bryan's age, Donnie was way too old for me. But he was so sweet and shy and so—

''But Barbara did invite him, didn't she?'' asks Nicky, like she's more just curious than really interested.

Of all the guys that Bryan palled around with when he was in high school, Donnie was the only one who ever looked at me like I was actually me and not just his friend's pain-in-the-ass little sister.

12

"She sent out the invitations," says April.

"But inviting him was Bryan's idea," says Lenny.

He'd talk to me, Donnie, and ask me what I was up to and what I was interested in—besides him, which I never told him, of course, but which he must have known. But he listened to what I had to say, and he asked questions about it, follow-up questions, like he really cared.

"Bryan and Donnie were best friends," Lenny reminds April, "before Donnie started going out with Barbara."

"And after," says Helen.

And sometimes, like when one of the guys hanging out with Bryan and Donnie would forget that I was hanging out with them too, and he'd tell some joke or make some remark that wasn't meant for innocent ears like mine to hear, when that happened and everybody laughed, I'd look over to see if Donnie was laughing too, and I'd see him looking back at me to see if I was, and I'd feel—for just that second when our eyes met—I'd feel like, "Maybe there's a way."

"I don't know who invited who," says Nicky Ambrose, adding her two cents to Lenny's penny, "but back home, they say that there's no better time than a wedding for putting ghosts to rest."

And other times, like the time up in Plainfield when Donnie pitched the famous three hitter that won Wildwood its first ever state championship, after the game was over when everybody piled onto the team bus for the ride back to Wildwood, I wound up sitting on Donnie's lap and pretended to fall asleep; and Donnie didn't want to wake me up, so I stayed like that, sitting on his lap with his arms wrapped around me and my head against his shoulder— the whole way home I kept telling myself, "There has to be a way!"

"Donnie P.," says April. "I still get goose bumps when I think of him, horsing around at the beach that day— Bryan's birthday, senior year.

"Remember?" she asks Lenny and Helen. "Those cut-offs he was wearing? When he came running out of the water? And they were all wet? And you could see . . . ?"

"Donnie Palomino!" Nicky volunteers.

Helen lets out a whoop.

"That's right!" April squeals.

"That's what we called him!" Lenny cries.

"Donnie Palomino!!" they scream.

It's more than I can take.

I say, "Excuse me. I've got to rehearse," and I head for the door.

"So," says Nicky, taking no notice of me, "do you think there's any chance that he'll come?"

"I doubt it." Lenny sighs.

April shakes her head and says, "No."

"*Naaaay!*" says Helen.

And everyone laughs.

And *bang!* says the door behind me.

FOUR

> *Dum-dum-dum-dum!*
> *Doobie-doobie.*
> *Dum-dum-dum-dum.*
> *Doobie-doobie . . .*

I don't think I would have showed up here today if Barbara Sweeney hadn't asked me to sing. Not that it was her idea. Bryan put her up to it, I'm sure.

But since I sang at both of my other brothers' weddings—Rollie, the state trooper, who's forty-two, and

Eddie, the treasury agent, who's thirty-six—and since Bryan, who's just twenty-one and sworn to be anything but an officer of the law, is the only one that I actually grew up with and the only one that I've been really close to, how could I say no?

Especially after the special way that Pop, when I told him that I wasn't going to any shotgun wedding, gave me the look that's supposed to make hardened criminals wet their pants and told me that I'd better cut the crap and shut my trap, if I knew what was good for me.

That, plus the whole family being here—Pop, Rollie and Eddie, their wives and kids; Aunt Peg, my mother's sister; and her boyfriend, Gene, from up in New York State.

And Mom, of course, who's here in spirit, even though we lost her four years ago, back when I was just thirteen. They say it's her that I get the singing from.

Bryan remembers Pop singing too, when Mom was alive, at weddings and parties and times when the families got together, but it's Mom's singing around the house that I remember.

In fact, in my best memories of her, Mom's out in the sun porch that my dad and brothers built for her off the kitchen one summer for her birthday, tending the dozens of houseplants that she rescued from the summer people— who abandoned them to fate when they left for home at the end of the season—nursing them back to life with healthy doses of sunshine and water and song.

I remember her in the kitchen, too, humming over her cooking, and in the living room with her knitting and in the backyard with her washing, humming to herself as she hung it out on the line.

It was like, wherever she went, Mom's music went with her, like she carried it inside of her, somewhere close to her heart.

It wasn't for show or to impress anybody. It was an inner music that gave her comfort and touched all of us who were close enough to hear it with a sense that every-

15

thing was exactly the way it should be, that there was nothing to worry about and no reason to fear.

In a way, it was like a cat's purring, Mom's music, and maybe that's why, wherever she went, even the most skittish cats would come out of hiding and find their way to her lap, as if they recognized her as one of their own.

The sad thing is, except for her music, the sound of her singing and humming, and her hands watering the plants and stirring the pots and pinning up the laundry, the only real pictures of Mom that I carry in my mind are pictures of her in bed, near death, wasted by the cancer that took her.

I don't even remember the last time that I saw her, because I was expecting to see her again, when one day at school I was called to the principal's office where I found Bryan, who'd come to fetch me, waiting for me with tears in his eyes. I'll never forget the way that he reached out and took my hand and told me, "She's gone to Jesus."

Bryan, the dumb bastard! If it wasn't for him, I wouldn't be here now, standing out on the Sweeneys' front porch, rehearsing, while all the happy people who arrived in all the shiny cars that are parked up and down the road on either side of the house are inside, mixing and mingling, chittering and chattering away and waiting for the slaughter to begin.

If it wasn't for him, I wouldn't be here with my shoes kicked off and my slippery blue bridesmaid's gown jacked up over my knees, strumming away on my air guitar and bopping along to this song that I'm making up in my head.

If it wasn't for Bryan, I wouldn't be thinking about treating the people inside to the World Premier of this song that I'm making up.

> *Dum-dum-dum-dum*
> *How could he be so—*
> *Dumb, dumb, dumb, dumb?*
> *He told her, "No,"*

But she was in a hurry,
Said he shouldn't worry,
Made his mind up quick as that.

Thought he was a smarty.
Now she's two weeks tardy.
Don't forget your Party Hat!

Party Hat! Party Hat!
Don't forget your Party Hat!
Party Hat! Party Hat!
If you're gonna' party!

"Everybody!"

Party-Ha—!

"What?!"
"Sorry," says Jim Sweeney, suddenly standing there, lying through his teeth and smiling a mile a minute.

"Great song!" he says.

My legs!

"Nice legs," he says.

I slam my knees together and shake and shove the hem of my gown down to the ground.

"What do you want?" I ask him.

"Not me," he says. "The people inside. They want an encore."

Teetering on one foot and wedging my other foot into a shoe, I say, "Ha!"

"They sent me to find you," he says. "Like a talent scout. Sort of. I'm the best man, you know."

"Yeah," I tell him, wedging my other foot into my other shoe. "And I'm the Queen of England!"

Wishing that I'd come up with something more devastating, but making the least of a bad moment, I turn on my heels and—with Jim Sweeney's laughter trailing behind me like a train—I head for the door.

FIVE

There's a thing called a Judas ram—that's this male sheep that they keep in the stockyards where sheep get sent to be killed and cut into lamb chops and stew meat and stuff.

The Judas ram, though, doesn't get killed. He just does his job, which is leading the other sheep into the slaughterhouse, and once he's got them all inside, he just turns right around and walks out and goes back to munching grass and enjoying his life, the same as he did before.

That's kind of what I feel like. I'm the first member of the wedding party to enter the big room, like a ballroom, where the wedding is going to take place, and even though the wedding procession isn't following right on my heels, as I slip into the back of the room and slide over to the piano, what I feel like is this sheep, this Judas ram.

In fact, as the piano player, Mr. Stanley—who used to be my music teacher when I was in junior high school and never thought much of my singing or me—looks up from the piano and greets me with a grudging smile, I'm thinking, *"Baa! Humbug!"*

"So soon?" he whispers.

"Afraid so," I tell him.

"Tra-lah," says Mr. Stanley, heaving a sigh that reeks of peppermint and alcohol and then, blazing a shortcut

18

from the middle of the piece that he's playing, he arrives in no time at all at its stirring conclusion.

And now, as their conversations, stripped of their underscoring, falter and fail, everyone turns and looks to the back of the room.

When they spot me, dressed in my bridesmaid's gown, sitting at the piano next to Mr. Stanley, they know the ceremony is about to begin.

Pop can't wait. I can see him dressed in his tuxedo and sitting with the rest of the family on the right side of the aisle in the first row of chairs facing the white latticework altar that the Sweeneys had set up for the ceremony.

As he cranes around to catch a look at the double doors behind me, his eyes meet mine, and if I didn't suspect he'd been nipping at the Jameson's I'd almost swear it was the sight of me, dressed up the way I am and looking for once like his idea of what a girl should look like, that's put the gleam in his eye and the smile on his lips.

For a second, as I return his smile, I wonder what my life with Pop would be like if I could just let myself be the girl he'd like me to be.

But then I remind myself that the girl my father would like me to be is my mother, the way that he imagines she must have been when she was my age—a girl so fine and fair that she never could have existed anywhere but in his imagination—a girl so perfect in every way that I could never hope to measure up to her.

"So what's the point?" I ask myself, as I feel the smile on my face turn false and grow heavy.

And now, as I notice Heloise Sweeney, the mother of the bride, slipping in the door at the front of the room and joining her family in the first row of chairs to the left of the aisle, the smile drops from my face. The moment of truth has arrived.

Mrs. Sweeney nods to Mr. Stanley, and Mr. Stanley, after taking a moment to compose himself, lifts his hands, wrists first, from his lap, dangles his fingers over the keyboard, and then, lifting up from his seat, he pounces down on the first chords of Wagner's the "Wedding March" and—*dah-dah-dah-dah*—the zombie parade begins.

Reverend Brewster leads the pack. Dressed like a hanging judge in a long black robe, he pops out of the double doors behind me and bobbles down the aisle, smiling left and right, as he makes his way to the altar.

The groom is next, Bryan, as handsome a horse's ass as you'll ever see, walking down the aisle, smiling like he hasn't a care in the world or a brain in his head.

Then it's "best man" Jim Sweeney. I shudder at the thought that he's about to become some kind of relative of mine, a very distant one, I hope, the more distant the better.

Rollie and Eddie are next. They come in side by side, leading Bryan's ushers—friends of his, guys that he grew up with—carrying memories of the boys they were behind their solemn faces.

Then Barbara's bridesmaids, dressed like me, in slippery blue satin.

Nicky Ambrose sets off a quiet riot when she enters. All the men and boys in the room feast their eyes on her and all the women and girls—turned to crumbs on the table of their escorts' imaginations—try not to notice.

It takes a moment before the stir subsides, and then it's another moment before—"Here comes the bride!"—Barbara Sweeney enters, looking—I have to be honest—better than I ever dreamed that she could. Better than Nicky Ambrose. Beautiful, in fact, like brides are supposed to look.

Dressed in a white taffeta gown, trimmed with fine lace, crowned with a diamond tiara and trailing a train of sheer white veil, she enters alone.

And then, as her father, Jock Sweeney, enters and takes his place at her side, she takes his arm and, riding a wave of murmured approval, they make their way down the aisle.

Bryan is waiting to meet them as they complete their journey and arrive at the altar.

Lifting his daughter's hand from his arm, Jock Sweeney places it in Bryan's hand and then steps aside.

And now, as Bryan helps Barbara Sweeney up onto the dais and takes his place beside her, I rise from my seat on the piano bench, turn to them, and start singing the song that Bryan and Barbara Sweeney asked me to sing, the same song that I always sing at Hanna family weddings, the song that was my mother's favorite—

> *"Drink to me only*
> *With thine eyes,*
> *And I will pledge*
> *With mine.*
> *Or leave a kiss*
> *Within the cup*
> *And I'll not want*
> *For wine. . . ."*

And as I sing, I'm looking around the room and noticing how, except for me, everybody here has somebody, some special somebody.

Like Rollie and Eddie have their wives, Marcy and Jenny, and their kids.

And Pop, who—although it's more than four years since he lost her—still has Mom.

And Bryan, the dumb bastard, who's got Barbara Sweeney.

And suddenly, I'm choking up!

Me! Hotshot Holly Hanna!

I'm singing, but as I sing, it's like I'm choking and tearing up so bad, I'm afraid I'm not going make it all the way through to—

21

> *"Drink to me only*
> *With thine eyes,*
> *And I will pledge*
> *With mine."*

As I hit the last note of the song, I see Bryan and Barbara glance at each other and, in their glance, I see the real love that they feel for each other.

And in the next moment, as I hold the last note of the song, like they're offering to share the real love that they feel for each other with me, Bryan and Barbara turn their eyes to me and, suddenly, my throat closes up and chokes off.

"Please rise," says Reverend Brewster.

As the crowd rises to its feet, I whirl around and, blinded by my tears, I duck my head and break for the door.

With no idea where I'm going, where to run to, or where to hide, I charge out of the big room, stumble across the front hall, and push out the front door.

Emerging into the brilliant sunlight, wiping the snot from my nose with the back of my hand, I race across the porch and—

"Hi, Squirt!"

Donnie!!

There he is, big as life, climbing the front steps and stepping onto the porch!

"No!" I scream, and without breaking stride I blow right by him and go flying out over the front steps.

Ooof!

I crash to the ground and rip my gown and skin my knees and the heels of my hands.

But quickly, before anyone can come to my rescue, I roll over and get to my feet.

I hike up my gown, and, kicking off the only shoe that I'm still half attached to, I take off running, as hard as I can—down the front lawn, across the road, over the beach,

22

and straight into the ocean—where I pitch myself, face first, into the water, close my eyes, and pray to God to take me.

SIX

Walking along the beach.
Waiting for my gown to dry.
And my hair.
And my eyes.
I can't believe my luck!
I mean, here I was, practically praying that Donnie would show up for the wedding and when he did and he saw me . . .
Is that you, Holly?! I wouldn't have recognized you! The last time I saw you, you were just a little girl. But now! Just look at you! You're so . . . so . . .
Stupid is what I am, for even dreaming there was a chance that a guy like Donnie would ever take a second look at girl like me.
And now that he's seen me at my worst, tear-assing out of the Sweeneys' front door, wailing and flailing around like some madwoman, nearly running him over, and then swan-diving onto the Sweeneys' front lawn, it's almost impossible for me to imagine him galloping in like Prince Charming, leaning down and lifting me up onto the back of his white charger, and riding off with me to the land of Happily Ever After.
Could I imagine him doing that before?
Yes.

Did I?

You bet.

Recently?

Would you believe today?

No.

Trust me.

But how in the world could a bright kid like me, living in a time like right now and a place like right here, walk around believing in a fairy tale like Donnie Pelligrino?

How could I not?

I mean, you've got to believe in something, don't you? In somebody? Like everybody needs somebody to love, don't they?

Which means that I've got a real problem.

Because the guys that I've met, at least most of them, it's not like they're another gender. It's more like they're another species.

I mean, some guys, as long as you don't like them, can be all right. But as soon as a guy finds out that you like him, even just a little, the game of live and let live is over and the game of give and get begins.

And the next thing that you know, you're in the back seat of some car, wondering why you're doing what you're doing with the guy you're doing it with, when you can't remember why you liked the guy in the first place.

So you break it off—the relationship, that is—and retire to your bed and what pleasures you can find there, under your blanket and in your head.

> *No, Donnie, don't!*
> *Oh, Donnie, do!*
> *Oh, Donnie! Donnie! Donnie!*
> *I love—*

"Holly-lu!"

Aunt Peg!

I hear her behind me, calling me by the name she always calls me, "Holly-lu," which is short, she says, for "Hallelujah!"

"Praise the Lord!" I answer, and, turning around, I discover Aunt Peg, wreathed in smoke from her smoldering cigarette, standing up above me where the beach begins its slope down to the water.

Trudging down the slope to join me near the water's edge, she says, "Hiya, darling," and throws her arms around me, gives me a hug, and kisses my cheek.

Then, holding me away from her, she looks into my eyes and gives me the smile that always reminds me of my mother.

"How's the water?" she asks me, straight-faced, as if I were standing there in a bathing suit, instead of a waterlogged bridesmaid's gown.

"Buoyant," I tell her.

"Shame," she says.

And that does it.

I break up.

And so does she.

And then she links her arm in mine and together we set out walking along the beach.

After we've walked a step or two, with her usual uncanny knack for getting to the heart of things, Aunt Peg says, "Isn't that your baseball player?"

Like I don't know who she's talking about or where she's coming from, I say, "Donnie?"

"Yes," she says.

"I think he belongs to the Red Sox," I tell her.

"Lock, stock, and oomph?" she asks me.

"I don't know about his oomph," I tell her.

"Shame," she says.

"Yes," I agree.

"Don't I remember a picture of him with his leg kicked up somewhere around his ear, stuck up on the wall in your room?"

"No," I tell her.

She looks over at me.

25

"On the back of the door," I remind her. "So if my door was open and he walked by, he wouldn't see it."

She nods.

"So that solves the riddle of why you ran out of the wedding as soon as you finished singing," she says.

I look at her.

"So you could be there to greet him, as he arrived," she says.

I laugh.

But she isn't kidding.

"I didn't know he was coming," I tell her.

She smiles like she knows better.

"You must have wished that he would," she says.

"Yes," I admit.

"And wished hard," she says.

"Yes," I tell her, "but you don't think—"

"That we get what we wish for?" she says. "Yes, I do. I'm sure of it."

"You believe that?" I ask her.

She nods.

"What your secret heart requires, it draws to it," she says like she's quoting from somewhere, some book or something, "just as surely as the moon draws the ocean."

"But what is it that my 'secret heart requires'?" I ask her.

"I don't know," she says. "That's a riddle for you to unravel. But unless it's a herring gull, you're not likely to find it here."

We've stopped walking now. We're just standing, looking out over the water, watching the tankers inching along the horizon.

"You don't think I'm going back there?" I ask her, nodding to the house across the road.

"Why not?" she asks me.

"After the way he saw me? He must think I'm a raving lunatic."

"So?" she says.

"So," I ask her, "what would I tell him? How could I explain?"

"Oh," she says, putting her arm around my shoulder, "don't worry about that. We'll think of something."

As she turns me around and begins steering me back across the beach to the house overlooking it, I ask her, "Like what?"

SEVEN

"LSD flashback," I explain.

Donnie Pelligrino looks puzzled.

Maybe it's my gown. Maybe he's wondering why it's no longer the same color as the other bridesmaids' gowns. But since he doesn't ask, I don't tell him that it got bleached by the sun and the salt water and scorched a little here and there by the iron that Aunt Peg borrowed from somebody in the kitchen and put to work smoothing out the wrinkles while I was in the shower washing the beach out of my hair.

"What do you mean?" Donnie asks me.

We're in the same room where the wedding took place, only now it's set up for the wedding reception that's bubbling and babbling all around us.

"When I was just a baby," I tell him, "Pop busted this gang of hippie drug dealers. Except for their leader, who got away. And one night, for revenge, this guy snuck into our house and found his way to the kitchen and laced my formula with LSD."

27

I pause for a moment, waiting for the lightning to strike me. When it doesn't, I continue.

"And ever since then," I say, "every now and then—and especially when I hear Grateful Dead music—I just, like, freak out, you know?"

Donnie just looks at me, like he's trying to decide if I'm being serious or just hacking around.

But Nicky, who's standing at his elbow, breaks out laughing.

At about the same moment as I'm thinking, *Thanks a lot!* Bryan chimes in.

"Don't believe a word of it!" he tells Donnie. "The thing that had Holly so shook that she couldn't stand it anymore was thinking about how much she was going to miss having her big brother around to wipe her nose for her."

Barbara's turn.

"Who says you're not going to be around?" she asks Bryan. "Once the honeymoon's over," she says to me, "we both plan to see a lot of you."

"If it's a babysitter that you're looking for . . ." says Pop.

"Not this year!" says Bryan, talking to Pop, but looking at me.

"You, Pop?!" asks Rollie, like he can't believe it.

"After the job you did, raising Holly?!" asks Eddie.

Everybody laughs and looks at me.

"Don't blame him!" I say.

Like he's pissed at me for making a liar of him, Pop shoots me a look, as he tells Eddie, "She turned out fine."

"Can we talk about something else?" I say. "Please? Because I'm starting to feel like a goldfish, you know?"

"Wet and slippery?" asks Bryan.

Ignoring him, I turn to Donnie.

"So, how's your arm?" I ask him. "Coming along?"

The way everybody looks at me, I feel like maybe, without my noticing it, all my clothes just dropped down

28

around my ankles and I'm standing there buck naked to the world.

"Holly!" says Bryan.

"No," says Donnie. "It's okay. Honest."

He turns to me.

"If you feel like a goldfish," he says, "just imagine how I've been feeling, with everybody afraid to even mention my arm. It's like the old story, you know? About the guy? The king or . . ."

"The emperor?" I ask him.

"Yeah!" he says. "With no clothes on. You know what I mean?"

I know what he means.

"Yeah," I tell him.

"I've been wondering when anybody was going to ask me about my arm," he says.

And he smiles at me.

And *God!*, when he smiles at me, I know what love feels like. And desire. And when both of them come together, it feels like—

"It's great!" he says.

Exactly! I think.

"All right!" I say.

He smiles, again.

"Yeah," he says. "I'm back on the roster Monday morning."

"Okay!" I say.

"And ready to start a week after that," he says.

Nicky gasps, swelling her ample bosom.

"Fabulous!" she says.

"That they are!" I think.

"You must feel like . . ." she says.

She cocks her head at Donnie, looks into his eyes, and grins.

"What *do* you feel like?" she asks him.

He looks at her for a second and that's all it takes.

"Dancing," he says.

29

She laughs and offers her hand to him.

"Love to," she says.

Without taking his eyes from hers, Donnie takes Nicky's hand, and saying, "Excuse us," he leads her off to the dance floor.

For a moment, through eyes blurred with tears, I watch them go, and then, before I *really* embarrass myself, I mutter, "Excuse me," and turn and hurry off in the opposite direction.

Toward the bar.

EIGHT

"Want to dance?"

"You talking to me?"

I want to make sure that I get it right this time. The last time Jim Sweeney asked me to dance—

"Yes," he says.

It's late.

Years have gone by since Donnie—

"I want to go home," I tell him. "You want to go home with me?"

"You've been drinking," he says.

"Do you?" I ask him.

I cock my head at him, look into his eyes, and grin.

"I've been drinking?" I remind him.

He looks at me for a second. "Do you need a ride?" he says.

I offer him my hand. "That's what I need," I tell him.

He sighs and shakes his head. "Meet you out front," he says.

And he turns and walks away.

"Like the rest of them," I think. *"Like Bryan."*

They were standing in the front hallway, Bryan and Barbara Sweeney, getting set to make a mad dash out the door, across the porch, through the crowd that was waiting to pelt them with rice, over to the driveway where a big black limousine was waiting to carry them off to the airport.

They hadn't noticed me standing at the entrance to the living room. They didn't realize that I'd hung back, waiting until the last moment to say—

" 'Bye, Bryan."

He turns. Smiling and opening his arms to me, he says, "Holly!"

I hurry over to him and fall into his arms, and so he won't notice that I'm crying, I bury my head against his chest and say the first thing that comes to mind, which turns out to be, "Have a good time."

He laughs. "I'll miss you, Holls," he says.

I hug him hard and tell him, "I love you."

And then, quickly, before I lose my nerve, I tear myself away from him and turn to Barbara.

"You, too," I tell her, just getting it out before I fall into her arms and hug her hard.

"Oh, Holly!" she says, hugging me back.

"All aboard!" says Jim Sweeney, as he arrives at the door.

"Here we go!" says Bryan.

" 'Bye," says Barbara, smiling at me through her tears.

Taking her hand, Bryan tells me, "I'll write to you from Paris."

As he leads Barbara to the door, the crowd outside bursts into applause. Pausing a moment at the threshold, he turns back to me, smiling and as happy as I've ever seen him.

31

"Au revoir," he says.

And then he's gone.

He's history.

My brother.

Bryan.

And Donnie.

He's history too.

He took off, right after Bryan did.

With Nicky.

I didn't say good-bye to him. I waved good-bye from behind the curtains of a window in the library.

He had told everybody, since they were both flying out of LaGuardia, he was giving Nicky a lift to the airport. But the way the two of them were grabbing at each other upstairs in the sewing room when I came across them while I was looking for a free bathroom a couple of minutes before they took off, I doubt that they got past the nearest motel.

So I watched them from the library as they climbed into the back of Donnie's limousine. And I watched Donnie's driver closing the door behind them.

And then, as he climbed in front behind the wheel and drove them away, I waved good-bye.

"Keep going." Jim Sweeney pulls into the driveway that runs around the side of my house. "Around to the back," I tell him.

He drives around to the back of the house and pulls to a stop in front of the garage.

He's driving a little sports car—his own, of course—the kind that you can reach across the front seat from behind the wheel and open the passenger door. Which, of course, is what Jim Sweeney does.

He leans across me and opens the door.

And then, he sits back up behind the wheel.

"You coming?" I ask him.

He hasn't switched off his ignition.

"Nobody's home," I tell him.

He shakes his head. "Pass," he says.

I look at him.

"You're drunk," he explains.

"I'm not!" I tell him.

"And you're—what?—sixteen?"

"Eighteen!"

"And a liar, besides," he says.

"If nobody knows," I ask him, "what's the difference?"

"The difference," he says, talking slowly, like he's talking to a kid—a stupid kid—or a drunk, "is the difference between my sister and me."

I look at him, like "Yeah . . . ?"

"I've always been happy," he says, "playing in my own backyard. But Barbara never was. She was always wandering off, looking for adventure on the other side of the tracks, the wrong side. Which might have been all right, if she hadn't let the strays that she picked up on her little outings follow her home—to my backyard."

I look him in the eye.

"If you mean what I think you mean," I warn him.

"I do," he assures me.

"Well, then," I tell him, my voice rising with every word, "I guess you'll just have to excuse Bryan and I—"

"Bryan and me," he says.

"—if we haven't got the breeding it takes to be a real pedigreed son of a bitch like you!"

Ending in a shout, I swing my legs out of the car, get to my feet, grab the car door, and slam it hard behind me.

Marching across the yard, I let myself in the back door and slam it hard behind me.

I stride across the kitchen, into the bathroom, and over to the toilet.

I bend to lift the toilet seat and puke—wine and lobster bisque—all over myself, the wall, and the floor.

NINE

No wonder! Look at you! Who'd want to go to bed with a hag like you? Even if you begged them?

Which you did. Admit it, slut! You threw yourself at Jim Sweeney. And he laughed at you, the bastard. He laughed at you because—look at you! Have you ever seen anything so pathetic?

And you thought that Donnie Pelligrino would—what? Love you? Want you? Why?! Why would anybody? How could anybody? Look at you!

Go ahead! Cry some more! Baby! Cry some more, and see what good it does you!

See who comes running to dry your tears! See if Bryan comes! Or Pop!

Pop! He could be home any time now. I can't let him see me like this! Not that he would. He'd just look right past me, or through me, like he always does and always has and always will! But still—

I tear my eyes away from the mirror over the sink in the upstairs bathroom.

I've just stepped out of the shower, where I was trying to wash off the smell of puke and Lysol that I brought upstairs with me after I cleaned up the mess down there.

But now, wrapping my towel around my hideous body, I switch off the light and pad down the hall to my room.

Once inside, I drop the towel on the floor, crawl into bed, and close my eyes.

In the dark, lying in my bed, I search my mind for a lullaby to comfort me and ease me down into sleep.

But after a moment, I find myself singing—

> *"Nobody likes me.*
> *Everybody hates me.*
> *Guess I'll go eat worms."*

TEN

I'm not a mutt!

I sit up in bed. It's the middle of the night. I haven't slept a wink. I've been lying here thinking, and that's the conclusion that I've come up with.

Just because Jim Sweeney says I'm a mutt that doesn't make me a mutt, any more than his saying that Bryan is a "stray" makes him a stray. It just so happens that Bryan's a hell of a guy and I'm a hell of a girl and Jim Sweeney is a dick.

And so is Donnie Pelligrino, I guess, if all that he's interested in is playing *Wham-bam! Thank you, Ma'am!* with boy-toys like Nicky Ambrose. That doesn't make me a mutt, either.

And anyway, who are these guys? I mean, who put this sniveling wiener and this preening jock in charge of telling me what I'm worth?

I did? By putting Donnie up on a pedestal?

I was young.

I did? By throwing myself at Jim Sweeney's feet?

I was stupid and drunk and hurting—and hateful, too, maybe, but never mind about that.

I climb out of bed. I can hear Pop, downstairs, snoring like a buzz saw. I grab a shirt out of the closet, an old work shirt of Bryan's that's soft with years of washing and hangs down to here. I put it on and tiptoe out into the hall.

I'm not a mutt. Now that I don't have Bryan around to remind me—even if I'm not gorgeous or brilliant or really gifted, I'm at least average or better in most ways that are supposed to count for something—I'll just have to keep reminding myself.

It's true, I'm not beautiful, like the girls in the Cover Girl commercials. And, so far, nobody's invited me to appear in the *Sports Illustrated* swimsuit issue. And MIT hasn't offered me a scholarship. Or the Geffen label, a contract. Or the Lakers, a signing bonus. Or the New York Philharmonic, a chair. Or the Nobel Prize Committee, even a simple thank you note.

But, hey! Nobody's perfect, right? But does that mean, since I'm nobody's Ideal Young Woman, that I should be treated like a mutt? Should anybody be treated like a mutt? Should mutts?

I mean, look at Joey Doyle. Not that he's a mutt. But my point is, right now Joey Doyle is hot and everybody in the world knows it.

But if you ask people around here, people who were about his age when he was coming up, most of them, if they remember him at all, will tell you—in looks, personality, brains, sports, skills, values, you name it!—he fell way short of nothing special.

They say, if anybody had told them that they'd be seeing Joey Doyle on TV someday, they wouldn't have believed it—unless it was for, like, botching the holdup of a convenience store with only six dollars in the till or something.

They didn't think Joey Doyle had much of a future. But, boy, were they wrong!

And me—they're wrong about me, too—people are, just like they were wrong about Joey Doyle.

I'm not a mutt. And I'm sick and tired of being treated like one. I'm sick of being ignored, and I'm tired of being abused. And if it means that I have to learn how to stand on my own two feet, if that's what it takes to get noticed and cared for and to sometimes be the one who gets to pick and choose, then I'm ready and willing to learn.

I mean, if Joey Doyle, coming where he came from, can do it, then why, since I'm coming from the same place, why can't—

Bryan! What a nice surprise!

Bryan's left me a present. A guitar. His guitar. The one that I've wanted for years but refused to take because I was hoping that someday he'd pick it back up again and go back to playing, but—*Wow!*—here it is in Bryan's room, up in the attic, propped up in the corner, leaning against the wall.

I pick it up and, quietly, so as not to wake Pop, I strum it to see if it's in tune.

Yes! I smile and settle onto the floor.

I lean back against the wall and cross my legs and rest the guitar in my lap.

I start strumming it, running through my four chord repertoire, searching for a tune, thinking about Joey Doyle and me and how, like him, but in my own way, *I*—

"Wanna be a rock 'n' roll star,
So tough, you never seen nobody tougher.
I wanna hear 'em screamin' when I play my guitar.
I wanna see the little boys suffer.
I wanna be a rock—
I wanna be a rock—
I wanna be a rock, rock, rock 'n' roll star.
Watch out!"

37

I'm writing a song!

"You call that a song?!"

I'm in the middle of writing a song, my first song on Bryan's guitar, my new guitar, when I hear this voice inside my head, asking me—

"Do you, Squirt?"

Squirt?!

I jerk my head up from the guitar, as if I actually expected to see somebody sitting there, and—

Oh, my God! I actually *see* somebody sitting there!

"Who the fuck are you?!"

He smiles.

"Who the fuck are you?" he says.

He's a young guy, about—I don't know how old, but—

"What do you want?" I ask him.

He's just sitting there, this guy—sitting on the floor across from me with his back against the wall and his legs propped up in front of him and his arms draped over his knees—and, still smiling, he looks over at me and says, "A little peace and quiet would do for starters."

Can you imagine?!

I mean, here's this guy who I've never seen before in my whole life, and who I've just caught doing I-don't-know-what in my brother's room in the middle of the night—and he's *complaining about my singing!*

"Then," he says, as if that wasn't enough, "if I could get you to put down that guitar . . ."

Guitar?!

Oh! Right! Bryan's guitar! When I looked up and saw this guy sitting there, staring at me—without even thinking about it, I jumped up on my feet and, grabbing Bryan's guitar by its neck, I hoisted it up over my shoulder where

I've got it now, cocked and ready to swing at the guy, if he so much as—

"Why the hell should I?" I ask him, meaning why should I put down Bryan's guitar.

"Because," he says, "I doubt that it will be much more use to you, using it as a weapon, than it was when you were using it as a musical instrument."

Do you believe this?!

"What are you?" I ask him. "Some kind of a break-in critic or something?"

He laughs!

Actually laughs!

"Funny," he says.

"Well," I say, "if you think *that's* funny—"

"But no," he says, shaking his head.

"Wait till you meet my father," I tell him, "the chief of police."

"I think I might be a ghost," he says, like he hasn't heard me.

"Crazy!" I tell him. "That's what you are!"

"Oh, yeah," he agrees. "Sure, I am. But what's that got to do with it?"

He laughs. "It's immaterial," he says. "And if I'm right, so am I."

"Bullshit!" I tell him.

"Okay . . ." he says, like he's about to prove it to me that he really is a ghost.

"Do you know anything about rock 'n' roll?" he asks me—as if he didn't see me, just a minute ago, sitting right here, writing and singing my own original rock 'n' roll song.

I just look at him.

"Did you ever hear of Jasper Rollins?" he asks me.

"Who?" I ask him, like I never heard of Jasper Rollins, which I haven't.

And he looks at me, like *"What planet are you from, anyway?"* and he says the name again.

39

"Jasper Rollins!" he says.

And I shake my head.

"Never heard of him."

"Never?!" he says, like he can't believe it.

"Are you deaf, too," I ask him, "besides dead and crazy?"

He doesn't answer. He just shakes his head, like he can't get over it, how I've never heard of this guy Jasper Rollins.

And then, like he's offering me a clue, he says, "You never heard—

"And she said—"

And he's starts singing. Up in my brother's room in the middle of the night, this guy that I've never seen before in my life starts singing—

"Call me Susan.
'Cause it's Tuesday,
And I hope we'll be friends.
I'll be Susan all night through,
Then I never will be Susan again . . .

"You never heard that?" he asks me.

But I'm not listening. I'm too busy thinking to myself, *"Wow! That was pretty! Sing some more!"*

"It was on the charts for weeks," he says. "Months!"

I shake my head and tell him, "Sorry."

Sorry?! Did I say, "Sorry?!"

"What about—

"Annie Moore don't live here anymore.
She couldn't stand the strain
The constant pain and sorrow.
Out the door, walked sunny Annie Moore.
And now we sure miss Annie Moore."

40

"Never," I tell him.

"Oh, come on!" he says.

Like he thinks I'm kidding him, when actually I'm thinking, *"Where is this guy getting all these great songs from?!"*

"Captain Hook recorded it," he says. "It was on the charts all that summer."

"Which summer?" I ask him. "And who's Captain Hook?"

He gives me this hopeless-case look.

"Captain Hook from *Peter Pan?*" I ask him.

He shakes his head like I got it wrong, and without telling me what's right, he just says, "Nineteen sixty-seven."

"Nineteen sixty-seven?!" I say it like it was a million years ago, instead of only a thousand. "I wasn't even born in nineteen sixty-seven!"

The guy looks at me for a second. Like it takes a second for it to sink in—that I couldn't have been born twenty-five years ago.

But then, nodding his head up and down like he finally gets it, he laughs and tosses his hair—which is dark brown and silky and which he wears down to his shoulders like some guys are doing now, but like everybody did in the sixties—out of his eyes and tilting his head to one side he smiles and says, "So when *were* you born?"

Okay, so he's cute, maybe even extremely cute, this maniac in my brother's room.

And so, all right, for a second I think about lying to him and telling him that I'm older than I actually am, because he seems to be.

But then I think, *"Wait a minute! Why am I lying to this guy who's pretending to be a ghost and is probably a rapist or a burglar or a housebreaker at best? I mean, what am I, nuts?"*

"Nineteen seventy-five," I tell him. "January fifteenth. Capricorn."

And like a guy who's buying a horse or guessing people's weights at a carnival, he looks me over, up and down, and says, "Then this must be about nineteen eighty—"

"Ninety-two!" I tell him.

"Which makes me seventeen," I add in my head, just in case he's bad at subtraction but good at reading minds.

But he isn't reading. Or listening, either.

"I was on a plane . . ."

He's talking to himself.

"A charter . . ." he says, like he's remembering—like he's been suffering from amnesia and all of a sudden his memory is coming back to him.

"We were flying to play a date . . ." he says.

"Where do you think you're going?" I ask him.

He's started unwinding himself, like he's getting up from the floor.

"At a club in Vancouver . . ." he says. "Me and Jann and Willie . . ."

"Hold it, right there!" I tell him.

"The new album was locked and mastered . . ." he says.

"Stop!" I warn him.

"We were getting set to tour behind it . . ." he says.

"I mean it!" I tell him.

"We needed to work out a little, get our chops together . . ."

He's up!

"Someplace off the beaten track . . ."

Six feet tall or more, he stands towering over me on these long lean legs that he's somehow managed to wedge into these tight, tight—*bell-bottomed jeans?!!*

"Aieee!!"

42

I swing the guitar at him, as hard as I can—and miss him by a mile.

Or possibly, the guitar passes clean through him, which . . .

But either way, as I go flying after the guitar—and bang up against the wall and nearly fall on my ass—I look back and see this guy standing right where he was, looking back at me and looking almost as surprised as I am, which is almost totally blown away!

And I say, "Oh, boy!"

And he says, "Yeah."

And I say, "Do me a favor?"

And he says, "You promise not to sing?"

"Walk over to the closet," I tell him. "Over there."

Without taking my eyes from his, I nod to the closet across the room.

He looks at it and then back at me.

"Okay," he says. And he turns and walks over to the closet.

"Open it," I tell him.

He looks at me.

Like maybe he's wondering if I'm planning to lock him up inside it—which I'm not.

"Please," I say.

He looks at me for another second, and then nodding, he reaches out for the doorknob, twists it, and opens the door.

"A mirror!" he says.

There's a full-length mirror mounted on the inside of the closet door.

"Don't move," I tell him.

With him standing there in front of the mirror, I ease over to a place behind him where I'll be able to see what he sees in the mirror.

"A little pale," he says.

"Oh, my God!"

"Or a little beyond it," he adds.

He has no reflection!
None!
I see no one in the mirror but myself!

"You're a ghost!" I say.

I feel a wave of terror—like ice water—washing over me.

He nods. "Of my former self," he says.

"Jasper Rollins?" I ask him.

"How do you do," he says, offering me his hand.

"Holly Hanna," I say and, reaching to shake his hand, I shake *thin air!*

I look at my hand and then at him.

"I can't believe this!" I tell him.

"Yeah," he agrees. "It's pretty far-out."

"Why are you here?" I ask him.

He shakes his head.

And then he shrugs and he looks me in the eye and he says, "Why are you?"

ELEVEN

Oh, my God! What—?

"Oww!"

What time is—?

Oo—my head!

Six-fifteen?!

God! I'll be late for—

Woo—no more wine for me, thanks!

God! I feel like I'm gonna—

"Jasper!"

I say it out loud.

Nobody answers.

Thank God!

He's gone.

Gone?!

Was he here?!

I sit up.

Oo—never again!

Bryan's room!

Right. I couldn't sleep. I was lying in bed, trying to sleep, but I couldn't because—

Oh, God! I propositioned Jim Sweeney!

God!

And he turned me down!

God! I could die!

I did die!

All over the bathroom.

But then, I cleaned up, and I showered, and I went to bed, and I couldn't sleep, so I put on Bryan's old shirt and—

Bryan's guitar! I've awakened, sprawled across Bryan's bed with my fingers curled around its neck. It's so beautiful and it's—

There!

I whirl around, terrified that I'll see him sitting—

Not there!

Thank God!

"Jasper" isn't there.

I laugh.

"Because he never was," I tell myself. *"It was a dream, stupid! It was—"*

"Was that closet door open before?" I wonder. "Or was it closed? Like it is, now?"

There was a song.

In the dream.

The guy in the dream sang—
Susan?

I'm Susan . . .

Or something.
Dreams—
Some of them stick with you.
But most of them, like this one—
It's like after you wash a frying pan and there's a drop
of water left in the bottom and you put it over a fire.
It's—*ssst!*—gone without a trace.
Except for the guy's face.
In the dream.
"Jasper," did I say? Yeah, *Jasper.*
Except for his face.
Which was nice enough, handsome even.
And his eyes.
Which were bittersweet, brown and haunting.
Yipes! Work! I can't be late for work!
I vault off the bed—
Bryan's bed! Don't ask me how I got there because I
don't remember, I swear!
But I hit the floor, and I take off running for the bath-
room, which is downstairs and which, I hope nobody's in,
because I've got to shower and get out of here. I'm work-
ing this morning at Avery's, helping out Carl, the cook,
while Mrs. Avery is off at the doctor's having her aching
back looked at.
*Bacon and eggs, pancakes and sausages, hot and cold
cereal, doughnuts and coffee, all you can drink for the
price of a cup. What'll it be, this morning?*
Thumping down the stairs from Bryan's room to the
second floor, unbuttoning Bryan's shirt as I go—so I won't
waste any time undressing once I get inside the bathroom—I'm trying not to think about how I feel. Because
I feel pretty awful.

Not just nauseous and headachy from last night's wine binge, which I deserve, but blue, too, because usually, if there *was* somebody in the bathroom at this hour—which I'm hoping there's not—but if there *was,* it would most likely be Bryan.

Except there's nobody in the bathroom.

Nobody but me.

I close the door behind me.

I lock it, and as I let Bryan's shirt slip off my shoulders and bend to scooch out of my undies, I'm thinking, even though it's hot in summer and cold in winter like attic rooms always are, since I've always loved Bryan's room with its slanted roof and gabled windows and all the little nooks and crannies and everything, now that Bryan's married and run off to Europe, what's to stop me from just hauling my stuff up there and moving right in? Especially now that I know it isn't haunted?

"Boo."

There's a face in the mirror over the sink, but it's only my face—my face, the way it looks when I'm hung over and *really scared!*

I swallow hard and catch my breath and hold it for a moment and then, praying no one will answer, I whisper, "Did somebody say, 'Boo'?"

No one answers.

"So I'm not completely crazy," I tell myself. *"Because I'm not talking to somebody who isn't there."*

"Or at least," I continue, *"somebody who isn't there, isn't talking to me."*

"Which means, if I am crazy," I'm somewhat relieved to conclude, *"I'm only really half—"*

I whip around and—

"Boo!"

Standing right behind me, towering over me, and smiling down at me, I see—

Aieee! Jasper Rollins!!

47

I scream my brains out!

"Aieeeee!!!"

Blam!

Pop slams through the door!

"Freeze!" he shouts.

I grab a towel to cover myself and scream all the louder—"Aieeeeee!"—as Pop drops into a crouch, extends his arms, grips his pistol with both hands, and fans the room with it.

"Freeze, goddamn it!"

"Pop!"

"Or I'll blow your goddamn—"

"No!"

"—head off!"

Pop looks over at me.

"No?!" he says.

Like I'm crazy.

"No!" I scream at him. "No! Go away! Get out!"

"But I thought—" he says.

"Get out!"

Holding on to my towel, holding on for dear life, I duck my head, drop my shoulder, plow into him—"Go away!"—and bulldoze him out the door.

Slam!

Damn!

Leaning back against the door, I close my eyes and take a deep breath and suddenly . . .

TWELVE

I'm back up in Bryan's room, looking at myself in the mirror on the back of the closet door, talking to the unreflected ghost of Jasper Rollins and telling him, "I'm here because I live here!" and asking him again, "Why are you here?"

He shrugs.

The ghost of Jasper Rollins shrugs and says, "Because I'm dead? Because the plane that I was flying in got struck by lightning and slammed into the side of a mountain and—'So long, Jasper'?"

"But why aren't you just dead, then? Like you're supposed to be?" I ask him. "Instead of here? Like this?"

Another shrug. "Beats me," he says.

Unfinished business! I think.

Like in this movie that I saw, or maybe it was a book that I read, but somewhere there was a ghost, an old guy, like a sailor or something, and the reason, it turned out, that he was a ghost, this sailor—why he didn't just die and pass over to the other side like everybody else—was that he had this "unfinished business" that he had to take care of before he could.

"What about it?" says Jasper Rollins.

"What about what?" I ask him.

"Unfinished business," he says. "You were saying . . ."

"I was?!"

I might have been.

"Uh-huh," he says.

I guess I was.

"What about it?" he asks me.

I try to remember how it went.

"There's something that you've left undone," I tell him. "Something too important to just leave that way, something that you've got to do before your soul can rest in peace."

He just looks at me for a second and then he breaks out laughing and shakes his head.

"Wrong!" he says. Like he's an expert, all of a sudden!

"No offense," he says. "But if that's the rule, then I've got to be the exception that proves it."

"Oh?" I say. "And why is that?"

"Well," he says, "because . . ." And he pauses, like he's about to break into a song.

And then, breaking into a song, he goes—

> *"I may have been just twenty-one*
> *By the time my time had come,*
> *But by then, little girl, I'd done it all . . ."*

He's got a great voice, all warm and smoky, like early morning sunshine peeking through a misty woods, and I hate to interrupt him, but—

"No," I tell him, "seriously . . ."

> *"Was there something that I missed?*
> *Some sweet thing I left unkissed?*
> *Not so far as I recall—I done it all!"*

I don't know if this song that's he's singing is something that he wrote before, something that just happens to fit the present occasion, or if he's actually making it up right on the spot. But it's a pretty good song either way, and he sings it really well.

Except when it's over, when he's finished singing this song, describing how the life that he led was so complete and so completely terrific that it left him without even a trace of "unfinished business," I just look at him and say, "Oh? Really?!"

"You can look it up in *Rolling Stone*," he says, with just a hint of pride peeking out from under his mostly bashful smile. "March 1966, *Jasper Rollins: His Lives and Loves*. It's pretty entertaining."

"I'm sure," I say. "But tell me—because I'd like to know—if you're not here to finish up your unfinished business then why are you here?"

He shrugs and says, "Because you sent for me?"

"Because I what?!"

"Because . . ." he says. And he does it again—pauses like he's going to break out singing.

And then he breaks out singing—

> *"You wanna be a rock 'n' roll star.*
> *So tough, you never seen nobody tougher.*
> *You wanna hear 'em screamin' when you play your guitar.*
> *You wanna see the little boys suffer.*
> *You say you wanna be a rock,*
> *Wanna be a rock—*
> *You wanna be a rock 'n' roll star . . ."*

And as he finishes—

> *"Yeah! Yeah-yeah! Yeah!"*

I sing right back at him—

> *"So what?"*

He laughs.
"You made a wish," he answers.
Which is a way of looking at it, I suppose.
"I suppose I did," I admit.

"And you meant it, right?" he says. "With all your heart?"

"Well, yes," I say. "I guess so, but—"

"Your wish has been granted," he says.

I look at him, like *"You expect me to believe that?"*

And I say, "It has?"

"You wanna be a rock 'n' roll star?" he asks me.

"Sure," I tell him, like *"Who doesn't?"*

"I can make you one," he says.

I look at him, waiting for him to tell me the rest of the joke.

But he just looks back at me.

So, okay—I say, "You can make me a rock 'n' roll star?"

"Well," he says, stepping back to take a good look at me, "within reason—and on a strictly local level—yes, I believe I can."

"Uh-huh," I say, like *"Tell me another one!"*

"Of course," he adds, "nobody can make a silk purse out of a sow's ear."

"Of course," I oink.

But he's so deep into looking at wretched me and trying to imagine the hot bitch that he's going to turn me into, he doesn't notice.

"But if you're willing to work really hard," he says, "and do what I tell you to do—yes, I'm pretty sure that I can turn you into something . . ." He searches for a word to describe the vision that he hasn't yet come up with.

"Or other," he concludes.

"Terrific," I tell him.

"Well," he agrees, "good enough for the purpose— which, if I remember, is—

> *"Gettin' some attention,*
> *Gettin' some affection,*

52

Getting what you're missin'
Thrown in your direction."

"Wasn't that it?" he says. "Isn't that what you're looking for?"

"More or less," I admit.

"Well," he says, "you're barking up the right tree."

"Woof!" I bark.

"I can show you how to go about getting what you're after," he says.

"Like you did?" I ask him.

He laughs.

"Not exactly," he says. "I mean, I busted through to where I was touring Europe with the Spoonful and toking with the Stones and fooling with the Countess Givernay."

He laughs.

"I couldn't understand a thing the Countess said, but *oo-lah-lah!*"

"French?" I guess.

"To say the least," he answers.

"And the money!" he goes on, "And the music! And the shows! A hundred thousand people hanging on your every word. Hundreds of girls waiting on your pleasure. And the clowns who used to treat you like a patch of dirt, coming up, eating their hearts out and practically dying of envy."

"And I can read all about it in *Rolling Stone?*" I ask him.

He nods.

"Among others," he says.

"And you can do that for me?" I ask him. "Get me some of what you had?"

"A taste," he says, "yes."

"By making me a rock 'n' roll star?"

"An iddy-biddy one," he says, "yes."

"Really?"

"Really."

"Why?"

"Why?!"

"Why would you?" I ask him. "Why would you want to?"

He shrugs.

"Well, for one thing," he says, "I'd have to be really good to pull it off."

The way he says it, like he's really thinking about it, I can see that he isn't saying it to insult me or to pump himself up. Even though there may be a little attitude in it, as far as I can tell, he's mostly saying it like he's seeing it.

"And besides," he says, "as long as I'm stuck here, with nothing else to do, why not?"

"And who's to say?" he goes on. "There's always a chance, if I can pull this off and get you what you wished for, maybe there will be something in it for me."

"Like a reward?" I ask him.

"Yeah," he says.

"You mean, like heaven?" I ask him.

He looks at me, like *"What are you, crazy?"*

"Me?!" he says.

But then, as he thinks about the alternative to heaven, the smile drops from his face and I'd swear he turns pale, as he says, "I've got to think about this."

"You're fading," I tell him.

Because, all of a sudden, I've noticed that he isn't just paling, he's also gone kind of gauzy—like I'm squinting to see him.

And yawning.

"You're fading, too," he says.

He's right. For a second I wonder if my fading has anything to do with his fading, but it's too much to think about. Suddenly, I'm so tired, it takes everything that I've got, just to say, "I'm tired."

As I turn away from Jasper, fading fast before my eyes, and stagger over to Bryan's bed, I hear Jasper's voice, like it's coming from a million miles away, saying, "You're tired? I'm dead!"

And then, as Bryan's mattress rushes up to greet me, everything goes black.

THIRTEEN

"**W**hat's going on up here?"

Through the bathroom door, I hear Aunt Peg chugging up the stairs from the first floor.

"How the hell should I know?" Pop barks at her. "I'm only the goddamned chief of police of this town for the last sixteen years!"

"Holly?" Aunt Peg calls to me through the door.

"She was screaming bloody murder in there!" says Pop.

"Something wrong?"

That's Gene, Aunt Peg's boyfriend—chugging up the stairs, bringing up the rear.

"Holly, darling?" Aunt Peg—on the other side of the door.

"I heard a scream," says Gene, arriving at the landing. "What's wrong?"

"I don't know," says Pop. "She never told me."

"Are you okay, Holly?" Aunt Peg asks through the door.

"Waiting till she's talked to her lawyer, I suppose," Pop gripes.

"Holly?" says Aunt Peg. "Are you okay?"

"Yes," I lie.

"Can I come in?"

"Just you?"

"Just me."

"Okay."

I have to pull hard to get the door opened because of the way Pop splintered the frame, when he slammed through it.

"Sorry, Pop."

As Aunt Peg slips into the bathroom, I see him through the crack in the door, standing out on the landing, shaking his head.

Leaning back against the door and pushing it shut, Aunt Peg takes a good look at me and then, "Mother of God!" she whispers. "If you don't look like . . ."

"Like I've seen a ghost?" I ask her.

She nods. "Just what I was thinking," she says.

I stifle a sob just long enough to say, "I have!" and then I burst into tears.

Aunt Peg throws her arms around me and hugs me to her and then, shaking like she's chuckling to herself and sounding more amused than alarmed, she says, "There, now! Nothing to get upset about. It runs in the family."

And while I chew on that, she turns and reaches out to the door, yanks it open, and calls out to the landing, "No need to worry about us. We're all right in here."

"Oh, you *are?*" says Pop, like *he's* not. "Then you won't mind telling me," he says, like he's pissed at Aunt Peg, who's got nothing to do with anything, "just what it was that set my little girl to wailing like a banshee in the middle of the night?"

"Not at all," says Peg.

"Holly saw a ghost and freaked at the sight. That's all."

That's what I imagine her saying.

But what she actually says—like it explains everything—is, "It's a woman thing."

"Oh!" says Pop, "Well, then . . ."

"She'll be okay now," says Peg.

56

And she pushes the door shut and winks at me and, like she's all excited for me, like I've just come in from a blind date or something, she says, "So what did he look like?"

FOURTEEN

"**I** think I lost the lottery again," says Aunt Peg, as I walk into the kitchen a few minutes later—after she's helped me get myself together enough to shower and dress and get downstairs on my own. "If I had three threes, I'd have noticed, wouldn't I?"

Wearing the embroidered red kimono that she wears as a housecoat, she's sitting on a stool that's pulled up to the counter in the middle of the kitchen, dripping ashes into her coffee and squinting at the morning paper.

"I'd think," I tell her.

Not a word about my seeing a ghost, which is just fine with me. I'd just as soon forget about the whole thing anyway, put it behind me.

"Boo!" he said, the dick—sneaking up behind me like that, while I was standing naked in the privacy of my own bathroom! "Boo!"

As I pour my coffee, Pop walks in the door. I don't know what I expect from him, probably that he'll be pissed about the door and want to make me pay for it, one way or another. But he doesn't seemed pissed at me at all or worried at all about the door.

He's actually kind of happy about it, happy that I gave him the chance to dash up the stairs and smash through the door and come to my rescue—not the kind of thing that he's done a lot of since a year ago when his doctor told him that he'd had a "silent heart attack," which I'm not supposed to know about, except that he told Bryan and Bryan told me.

"God!" I think. *"I could have killed the old bastard! And he's the only old bastard I've got!"*

But still, as grateful as I am to see him alive—and not kicking for a change—it's hard for me to feel a lot of sympathy for a man who hears his only daughter screaming bloody murder and, when he's told that her problem is a "woman problem," never asks another thing about it, but just turns and walks away like he doesn't give a damn.

Bryan says its because of Mom that Dad can't stand to deal with me—because I remind him of her and the memory is still too painful for him to bear.

But I don't care—because Mom's dead and sainted and I've got a whole life to live and where is he when I need him? Off protecting and serving everybody in town but me, that's where! So—

"Don't you have to be somewhere?" says Aunt Peg.

"Oh," I say, "yeah."

Looking at the clock on the wall above the kitchen sink, I see that it's already five of seven and, since I'm supposed to be at Avery's by 7:15, I think, *"Yipes! I've got to get out of here!"*

But now that I think about saying good-bye to Aunt Peg, who will be gone, headed back up to New York state before I get home from work today, I wonder what she could tell about me about ghosts if I had the time to listen.

But since I can't be late for work—

"Let's go then," she says.

And before I can point out to her that, except for her red kimono and the slippers on her feet, she isn't dressed—Aunt Peg's up from her stool, grabbing for her cigarettes, and headed out the door.

And me—

" 'Bye, Pop!"

I'm two steps behind her and—" 'Bye, Gene!"—out of here!

FIFTEEN

We walk along the beach—me in my jeans and tank top, Aunt Peg in her red kimono. It's the fastest way to go and the prettiest by far—although when the wind is up, like it is today, and the waves are pounding against the shore, you have to almost shout to be heard above the wailing of the one and the thundering of the other.

"And he said he was Jasper Rollins?" Aunt Peg calls over to me.

I nod. "You know who he was? Or *is?*" I call back to her.

"Both," she calls.

"Both?"

She nods and, moving over beside me, she puts her arm around my waist and falls into stride with me.

"He *was* a singer and a songwriter," she says. "And he *is* a ghost."

"Then he's real?"

"Seems like," she says.

"And not just—"

"Another LSD flashback?" she asks. She laughs and shakes her head.

"Nope," she says.

"And I'm not just crazy?" I asked her.

"You mean in general?" she says. "Or just about this?"

"About this."

"Nope."

I heave a sigh.

"Oh, come on!" she says. "Lighten up! He's nothing to be afraid of. Not now, anyway."

I look at her, waiting for her to tell me, besides singing and writing songs, Jasper was also a serial killer.

"When he was still flesh and blood, though," she says, "if you can believe what you read in the papers, he was pure hell on the ladies."

I shake my head, like I can't understand it.

"I guess, back in the sixties, they went for tall handsome guys with silky hair and soulful eyes," I tell her.

"Simpler times," she says, confirming my theory with a nod. "But I'm sure your ghost is no better or worse than any of the others that have appeared to the O'Neal women down through the years."

And then she goes on to tell me how the women in our family—my mom's and hers and mine—how they've been seeing ghosts, at least some of them have, since way back before her mother's mother first came to this country from the other side.

"As far back as anyone can remember," she says.

"Have you?" I ask her. "Ever seen a ghost?"

Like she regrets it, she shakes her head and says, "Not yet. But my cousin Sheila, out in California, has. And Margaret Anne, up in Boston. And her mother, Elizabeth. And going back, there was Aunt Dorothy Todd and the sisters, Alice and Audrey. Kinsolvings, they were. And, oh, on and on."

"My mom?" I ask her. "Did she see ghosts?"

"Your mom?!" says Aunt Peg. She laughs at the idea.

"The only ghost that Mary Katherine would ever let herself believe in," she says, "was the one that her church approved of."

"You mean, the Holy Ghost?"

Aunt Peg nods.

"As if all the other ghosts out there, all the thousands

and thousands of poor restless souls out there, were *un*-holy!" she says.

"Which they're not?" I ask her.

"Heavens no!" she says. "Well, maybe some of them are or get to be. But none that I know about from the family. They've always been just poor troubled creatures, plagued by poor troubled souls that wouldn't let them rest in peace."

"Because they've had unfinished business to take care of?" I ask her.

She looks at me.

"Stuff that they had to get done?" I ask her. "Before they could move on to wherever it is that they're going?"

"The next life," she says. "Yes."

"That's what I told him," I tell her. "That's what I told Jasper."

"Well," she says, "you told him the truth then. At least according to the way of thinking that's been passed down through the family.

"As close as we've been able to figure out, a person becomes a ghost if he dies without fulfilling his life's destiny and, instead of just being sent back to try it all over again in a different incarnation in another time and place, he's given this one last chance."

I nod and say, "Huh?"

Aunt Peg laughs and tries again.

"Before our souls can move on—up to heaven, if that's what you believe in, or just onto another life that's further along on the path to transcendence, if that's what you believe—we have to fulfill our life's destiny."

"Oh," I say. "Which is what? Our 'life's destiny'?"

"It's the same for all of us," she says. "Jasper and you and me and everybody else—in each lifetime, every soul needs to love and be loved, to know the sorrow of a love that isn't meant to be and the joy of a love that's returned in kind."

So I'll remember it, I try repeating it.

61

"To love and be loved," I say. "And—"

"To know the sorrow of a love that isn't meant to be," says Aunt Peg.

"And the joy of one that is," I add.

"Right," she says. "Or you're left with unfinished business."

"Which makes you a ghost," I say. "If you're lucky enough to get a second chance to finish up your unfinished business before you're sent back."

"Exactly," she says.

"So Jasper's really lucky," I say.

"Yes," she says, "and so are you."

"Me?"

She nods. "If you can help Jasper," she says, "if you can help him fulfill his life's destiny, so he can move on to the next life, it will be a blessing to you."

"And if I can't?" I ask her.

"The longer he's stuck between lives," she says, "the more likely he is to stay stuck."

"And haunt me?"

She nods.

"Like a bad reputation," she says. "Is that it?"

"Is—?"

As she slows to a stop and points up the beach, I follow her gesture to the start of the boardwalk and the run-down hot dog stand that looks out on the ocean from under a faded sign that reads AVERY'S BEACHSIDE RESTRANT.

"Your place of employment," she says.

"Oh! Yes," I say. "We're here."

"Here and gone," she says, taking my two hands in hers and giving me that smile that reminds me of my mother. "So, you'd best make hay while the sun shines."

I smile back at her and, loving her with all my heart, I say, "Make hay?"

She laughs and hugs me and translates for me. "Get busy!" she says.

And she kisses me and looks into my eyes for a moment

62

before she turns and walks away with a cloud of smoke billowing about her head and her red kimono flapping in the breeze.

SIXTEEN

I've got the radio tuned to WJRZ-FM, "Rock Solid," which I can't get away with when Alice is around, but which Carl doesn't mind my listening to when she's not.

Eric Clapton's singing *Bell Bottom Blues,* so sad it could break your heart because—according to this guy that Don Harmon, the disk jockey's been talking to—at the time Clapton wrote the song, he was in love with Patti Boyd, this beautiful model, who was married to George Harrison of The Beatles, who was his best friend.

So, I'm thinking, life's tough, even for rock stars like Eric Clapton.

And I'm waiting for Carl to dish up a stack of pancakes and a side of bacon for old Henry Vandergroot, who used to work on the railroad, once upon a time.

And I'm checking to see if anybody at the counter needs a refill on his coffee.

And I'm wondering, *"If Jasper Rollins is real, like Aunt Peg says he is, does that mean that he really can make me into a rock 'n' roll star, even an iddy-biddy one, like he says he can?"*

I'm getting to the point where I'm thinking, *"Maybe, he can!"* when Carl calls out, "Pick up!" from his spot behind the grill.

I put down the coffeepot, head over to the service

counter, pick up Henry Vandergroot's order, carry it over to Henry, and set it down on the counter in front of him.

"Syrup?" I ask him.

"Thank you," says Henry.

"Coming up," I tell him.

"I still say that bone-cracker that Alice is seeing is doing nothing but stealing her money," says Carl, holding forth from his grill, like a preacher from his pulpit. "There's nothing wrong with Alice that the love of a good man wouldn't fix up fast.

"And she's not so old yet," he says, "or so ugly, either, that she couldn't still get herself a man, if she wanted to. But you see now, Mr. Stiles, that's the whole point of the thing, of Harry's curse."

Harry's curse! Jasper's ghost! What is this—Halloween?!

"Uh-huh," says Mr. Stiles—Isaiah Stiles—who isn't listening to Carl any more than Carl is talking to him, but who doesn't mind cooperating with the pretense, so long as it doesn't interfere with his reading of this morning's *Wall Street Journal* and seeing how his stocks and bonds are doing.

"She never even had a backache until Harry up and died," says Carl. "It was Harry that had the bad back. But then he dies and all of a sudden she's got it. Now, you tell me that ain't Harry's way of making sure she don't go out dancin' with nobody else."

"Yup!" says Mr. Stiles.

"Haunting her from the grave," says Carl.

And old Helen Vogel, who spends her days on the boardwalk painting seascapes, one after another, that look so much alike it would take an experienced sea gull to tell one from the next, looks up from her usual bowl of oatmeal and raisins and says, "Maybe, instead of a chiropractor, Alice ought to be seeing an exorcist."

Sitting beside her, Stuey Ahrens, who's this really quiet kid that I know just barely from school—and even less than that from the Cobblestone where he works as the house roadie—Stuey cracks up.

And when I see him nearly spitting up his coffee, I crack up too.

But Carl says, "No fooling!" and he tells Helen Vogel, "You find me one that'll take Medicaid, and I'll drive her straight to him. Pick up!"

Who you gonna' call?

With the theme from *Ghost Busters* running through my head, I fetch an order of whole wheat toast from the service counter and carry it over to Laird Griffiths, this superjock friend of mine and Claudia's who, because she jogs the beach every morning with Claudia, tells everybody that she's Claudia's "personal trainer."

"Another soda?" I ask her, seeing that she's almost finished with the club soda that I brought her when she and Claudia first pulled in, a couple of minutes ago.

"No, that's okay," she says.

"Claudia?"

"I'm fine," she says.

She isn't eating. She hardly ever does, more than a taste of this or that, washed down with a sip of this or other, like the orange juice that she's drinking now. It's how she keeps her skinny-but-wow figure.

"So, what did he say?" I ask her.

"Who?" she asks me, like she doesn't know—like this isn't the way that I've been starting all our conversations for the last couple of weeks, since the first night of the Playoffs.

"Terry Kincaid," I tell her. *"The Leader of the Pack."*

"Oh," she says.

"When Eddie asked him about you joining up with Bent and playing in the Showdown?"

She gives me this look, like *"Do I really have to put up with this again?"*

"Eddie didn't ask Terry?" I guess.

Claudia shakes her head.

"Because you didn't ask him to?" I guess again.

She nods.

"Yes, you did?" I ask her. "Or yes, you didn't?"

She sighs. "If it ain't broken . . ." she says.

"But you said yourself," I remind her, "with you sitting in, playing the congas and mariachis—"

Claudia laughs. "Maracas," she says.

"Whatever," I tell her. "You said that the band sounded twice as good."

"Yes," she admits, "but—"

"And it must have looked a thousand times better!" Laird chimes in.

Claudia laughs.

"And Terry said—"

"That was just the one time," says Claudia.

"—that you were terrific!"

"At a rehearsal," she says. "And Terry was just being nice."

"Terry Kincaid?!" I ask her, like *"You expect me to believe that?"*

"Forget it!" she says, looking from one of us to the other, "I mean, come on, you guys!

"Why would Terry want to change the lineup for the Showdown, when the bunch of them are only now just getting over the party that Arthur threw for them, back on the night that they won the Playoffs?"

Like I didn't hear her right, I squint at Claudia and say, *"Arthur* threw the party?"

"Yes," she says. "I told you."

I shake my head and tell her, "You didn't say that Arthur threw it. You said he was there. But he *threw it?"*

Like all of a sudden, she's not so sure, Claudia says, "I think so."

I look at over Stuey Ahrens, sitting across the way. If anybody would know whether Arthur threw a party for Bent that night, it would be Stuey, since—as the Cobblestone's roadie—he'd have gotten stuck with all the dirty work.

66

"Stuey?" I say.

Not sure that he wants to own up to the fact that he's been eavesdropping on our conversation, Stuey takes a second before he nods and says, "Yeah. Champagne and everything."

I don't get it.

"I thought Arthur only did that for the band that's won the Showdown."

Stuey shrugs and says, "He does. Usually."

I look at Claudia.

She shrugs. "Don't ask me," she says.

"Weird," I say.

"Yeah," she agrees.

"But anyway," I continue, "all I'm saying is, you're too good to not be playing."

Smiling like she's flattered, but shaking her head like she knows better, Claudia tells me, "I'm not that good."

"I've heard you!" I remind her—which I have, at her house, knocking around her father's congas and bongos and whatnots.

"Fooling around," she says.

"Come on!" I tell her. "You're as good or better than half these clowns that you hear thumping away behind the bands over at the Cobblestone. Right, Stuey?"

"Huh?" says Stuey, who's gone back to pretending that he isn't listening to us.

"Don't you think Claudia should join up with a band?" I ask him.

"I don't know," he says.

"How should he know?" asks Laird.

"There's been girls in some of the bands," Stuey continues. "Not this year, so far. But I remember last year, a girl played keyboards with a band. And there've been singers, backups and leads."

"Any of them ever get anywhere?" Claudia asks him.

"No," he says.

Claudia looks at me and shrugs.

"There you go," she says.

"Damn, now! Look at this," says Carl. "Worse than she was last night."

It's Alice that he's talking about, Alice Avery coming down the boardwalk, looking twice her fifty-plus years, moving fast but listing badly.

"Ow!" I say. It hurts that much, just to look at her.

"She'll want her tea," Carl reminds me.

"Coming up," I say.

I turn to fetch her a cup of hot water from the pot on the hot plate, a wedge of lemon from the fridge, and one of her special Swee-Touch-Nee tea bags from under the counter.

"Holly!"

Before I've got it all together, she's arrived.

"Coming up!" I tell her, ignoring how cross she sounds, putting it down to the pain that she must be feeling.

"What is that?"

I've got it together now, and setting the makings down on the counter before her, I tell her, "Tea."

"No," she says, looking toward the end of the counter and staring daggers at the radio that's sitting there. "That!" she says.

I'd forgotten about that, about the radio, that I had it turned on and tuned in to WJRZ-FM.

But I remember it now.

"Oh!" I tell her. "It's—"

". . . I'll be Susan all night through,
Then I never will be Susan again . . ."

It sounds familiar, but—
What is that?!
"Jasper Rollins," says Stuey Ahrens.
Good grief!!
"Well, turn it off!" says Alice.

It is Halloween!
"Yeah! Sure! Sorry!" I tell her.
Who you gonna call?
I hurry to the end of the counter, reach for the radio, and switch it off.

> *"I'll be Susan all night through . . ."*

But it doesn't seem to go off.
So I switch it back on.

> *"Then I never will be . . ."*

But now there are two voices!

> *"Susan, again."*

And both of them are—
Jasper!
Suddenly, he's standing right there, leaning against the counter, grinning at me, and singing along in perfect harmony with himself!

> *"Hello, Sue!*
> *How are you?*
> *I am, too."*

"Turn it off!" cries Alice.
"Scram!" I tell him.
"What?!" says Alice.
"Okay!" I tell her.
I switch the radio off.
And Jasper disappears.
"God, I hate that stuff!" says Alice.
I heave a sigh and shake my head and, talking to myself, I say, "You don't know!"

SEVENTEEN

It's just like he said. In his time, Jasper was pretty hot stuff—writing chart songs and hits for himself and his friends, chasing around the US and Europe with the giants of his time, opening shows for The Jefferson Airplane, The Kinks, Buffalo Springfield, Delaney and Bonnie and rapidly approaching the time when he'd be the headliner and somebody else would be opening for him.

Audiences—guys and girls, but girls in particular—took to his "good-time music," to his "anytime attitude," and his "mannish-boy good looks."

His hard rockers and sweet love songs "brought guys to their feet and girls to their knees."

Wherever he traveled, whenever he played, he left behind him "fresh legions of believers and a trail of broken hearts."

"Just like I said, right?"

"Aaagh!" I scream.

"Shhh!" Jasper shushes me.

"Yes? Hello? Are you all right?"

The librarian comes looking for me.

"Now you've done it!" says Jasper.

"Me?!"

"Yes!" says the librarian. "You!"

"I saw a rat," I tell her.

Why lie?

"Oh! I see," she says, like she isn't surprised!

Rats? Here? In the stacks of the public library?

"Are you all right?" she asks me.

"I think so."

"It's an old building," she says.

"Yes."

"We do our best."

"I'm sure."

"But with all the cutbacks . . ."

"Yes."

"Please don't mention it to anyone."

"I won't."

"Well . . ."

"Thank you."

"You're welcome. And if you should see another . . ."

"I'll try not to scream."

"Thank you."

"You're welcome."

She turns and walks away.

"A rat, huh?" The second she's gone, Jasper's back.

" 'Running through girls like party snacks!' " Keeping my voice to a whisper, so as not to attract any more attention, I read to him from the bound copy of the March 1966 *Rolling Stone*, which I've pulled down from a shelf. " 'Gobbling them up by the handful.' "

"I was hungry!" he explains with a shrug and a grin.

"You were a rat!"

"I was young!"

"You didn't get much older!" I point out to him. "Or any nicer! You aren't now! You weren't this morning when you popped up, uninvited, at work! And you weren't before that when you popped up, uninvited, in my bathroom!"

The madder I get, the more he grins!

"Like a Peeping Tom, for God sakes! I mean, ghost or no ghost, just where do you get off, pulling a stunt like that?"

"You thought that you'd been seeing things," he explains.

71

Like he was doing me a favor!

"I *had* been," I tell him, "until . . . You don't know what it's like. You're standing there, looking in the mirror. Somebody says, 'Boo!' You turn around—"

"And what do you see?" he asks me, smiling and smug, like he's Perry Mason and he's finally backed me into a corner where I have to give him the answer that he wants to hear.

The hell I do!

"I see a *rat!*" I tell him—him and the rest of the world.

"Miss!"

Including the librarian.

"You promised!" she reminds me.

I must have been shouting!

"I—"

"Out!" she says, pointing to the door. "Now!"

EIGHTEEN

I'm heading home.

Skirting a crowd of happy campers—thumping volley-balls on the beach, jogging along the shoreline, cavorting in the waves—I'm skulking along a barren stretch of beach, like a bedouin in a sandstorm when I hear this voice behind me, calling "Holly! Wait up!"

I turn around and—*Him again! Give me a break!*

I turn and resume my homeward skulk.

"Holly!"

I imagine him behind me, slogging through the sand in his high-heeled cowboy boots, trying to catch up with me.

I smile to myself and pick up my pace.

"Hi," he says, popping up, right in front of me.

I stop short.

"What do you want?" I ask him.

He smiles. "I want you to have what you want," he says.

"What I want?" I ask him.

"Yes," he says.

"What I want," I tell him, "is for you to get lost."

And I step around him and continue on my way.

"I don't think so," he says, a minute later, suddenly walking next to me, carrying his boots, now, swinging them by their boot straps and matching me stride for stride.

"Why should I care what you think?" I ask him.

"Because I'm the guy who can get you what you really want," he says.

I look at him.

"Which isn't for me to get lost," he says.

"It isn't, huh?"

"No," he says. "It's for you to get found."

"Really?" I say.

"Except you're afraid—"

"I'm not!"

"—if you got up the courage to poke your nose out of the hole that you've been hiding in, you'd get found *out!*"

"Cute!"

"You're afraid—"

"I'm not afraid!"

"—if you gave the rest of the world a chance to see what you're really made of, they'd pretty soon come to realize that you're exactly as worthless and hopeless as you already know you are."

"I am not afraid! Or worthless! Or hopeless, either!"

"You just know your limits?"

"That's right."

"And you've already reached them, so . . ."

"So why should I believe in you anyway?" I ask him.

"It isn't me that you've got to believe in."

"Yes, it is!" I insist.

He looks at me.

"Just because you're Jasper Rollins," I tell him, "just because you *were* Jasper Rollins, and Jasper Rollins was a rock 'n' roll star, how does that prove that you can make me into—a silk purse?"

He laughs. "I'm sorry about that," he says.

"Great," I tell him. "But when you tell me that you're going to turn me into an overnight sensation—"

"Well . . . ," he says.

"Why should I believe you?"

He shrugs and asks me, "What have you got to lose?"

"A lot!" I tell him.

"Like what? Your invisibility?"

Ow!!

"Forget about me, okay?"

"Okay," he says.

"Forget what I think."

"Okay."

"What is it that makes *you* think that you're some kind of fairy tale genie, who can just pop out of a bottle and grant me my wish and make my dream come true?"

He smiles. "I made my dream come true," he says.

"Did you?" I ask him.

I'm thinking, *"If that's true, then why are you here? Why would you have been given a second chance, if you didn't have to finish up some unfinished business?"*

I'm think about the blessing, too—the one that Aunt Peg said would be waiting for me. I'm wondering if the baby rock stardom that Jasper is promising me might not be the reward I'd get if I helped him finish up his unfinished business.

"Yes, I did," says Jasper. "I made my dream come true. And you can do it, too, with my help. And you know it.

"So, how about it? Are you just jerking yourself around

here? Yourself and me? Or were you serious when you said that you want to be a rock 'n' roll star?

"Because, if we're going to pull this thing off, it's going to take time and effort and—God knows!—as good as I am and as much as I know, given what I've got to work with, more than just a little luck."

"Has anyone ever told you how truly obnoxious you can be?" I ask him.

He smiles. "Yup," he says.

"Well, whoever it was," I tell him, "they were right."

He nods. "On the other hand, has anyone ever offered to make your dreams come true?" he asks me.

Although I hate to admit it, especially to myself, it's the sad truth that I tell him when I shake my head and answer him, "No."

"Well?" he says.

And he waits for my answer.

And after a moment, I give it to him.

I slow to a stop and I turn to him and, looking him straight in the eye, I tell him, "I want to be the first girl ever to win the Showdown at the Cobblestone."

And he smiles—the ghost of Jasper Rollins smiles at me—and he says, " 'Atta girl!"

NINETEEN

I'm standing in the center of the room, Bryan's room, while Jasper is circling around me, cocking his head this way and that, taking mental snapshots of me and verbal potshots at me.

"All that hair!" he says. "When you bow your head like that you look like an Afghan hound."

"Bitchin'?" I ask him.

"No," he says. "Just telling it like it is."

He's taking an inventory of my assets, looking hard at the "raw material" that he's got to work with, before he sets to work turning me into a rock starlet.

"You think that you're showing off your hair," he says, "but you're really hiding behind it. Let's see what you've got to hide."

"Ah!" he says. "I like your eyes."

"Swell," I tell him.

"But how many eyebrows are you supposed to have?"

"Two," I tell him.

"We'll have to get a weed eater in there," he says. "Mascara?"

"No habla Espanol," I tell him.

"Eyeliner? Blusher? Lipstick?"

"Bingo!"

"Lipstick?"

"Cherry red," I tell him.

"Just?"

"If I haven't lost it," I tell him.

"Have you?" he asks me. "Lost it?"

He's stopped circling now. He's standing right in front of me.

"Are you asking me about my lipstick?" I ask him.

He shakes his head and says, "No."

"Do you think it's any of your business?" I ask him.

"Yes," he says.

"How?" I ask him.

He shrugs and says, "It helps if you know a little something of what you're singing about."

"Is that what I'm singing about?" I ask him. "Sex?"

"If you're singing rock 'n' roll," he says, "yes."

I look him in the eye and, coming in somewhere between Cher and Chastity, I tell him, "I know a little something about it."

He grins.

And then he says, "Play me something."

I glance at Bryan's guitar, sitting over in the corner.

"I don't really play all that well," I tell him.

"I remember," he says.

"What do you want to hear?" I ask him.

I go to get the guitar.

"Anything," he says. "But nothing original, okay?"

"Fast or slow?" I ask him.

"The faster, the better," he says.

" 'Hot to Trot'?" I ask him.

"Is that a question?" he asks me.

"A song," I tell him.

It's the song that Eddie Ballard's band, Bent, won the Playoffs with, the one that Eddie calls *The Slut Song* because—like he told Claudia—"It's hot and dumb and easy to get into."

As I settle down on the floor, set Bryan's guitar in my lap, bow my head down over it, take a deep breath, and begin strumming, I'm hoping Eddie's right about the song's being easy to get into because I'm not feeling superconfident about my carrying the day on sheer talent.

So I strum for a while and then, since I can't keep strumming forever, I look up at Jasper, who's standing across from me, waiting for me to get on with it, and I say, "Ready?"

"As I'll ever be," he says. "The question is—"

I know what the question is, so I don't wait to hear it. I just jump in with—

> "Some girls, they stop at nothing.
> They give you all they got.
> And other girls, they ask you 'Why?'
> But this girl says, 'Why not?'
> So . . .

77

It's no wonder, since she came,
Everybody knows her name.
Once she's started, she can't stop.
She's—
> *You know what?*
> *Hot to trot . . .*

Where other gals say, 'Cut it out,'
She'll tell you, 'Thanks a lot!'
> *It doesn't matter what you've—"*

"Okay!" he says.

Okay?!

"That's enough?" I ask him, half worried, half relieved.

"Oh, yes!" he insists.

I'm not crazy about the way he says it, but when he says nothing more, I have to ask him, "Well . . . ?"

"Well," he says, "it could be worse."

Like I'm bowled over by his enthusiasm, I say, "Wow! It could?!"

"You can carry a tune," he admits.

"Amazing, huh?"

"And you're not that bad to look at."

"I blush!"

He laughs.

"But if you walked out onto a stage with that little choir girl voice of yours," he says, shaking his head at the thought, "and all that hair and your eyes, gone to waste on a face with fewer highlights than a bowl of oatmeal—"

"Without raisins, I assume?"

"Even if you were dressed like a girl," he says, "instead of like a shortstop . . ."

He shakes his head again.

"You'd just fade right into the back wall," he says. "I can see you now . . .

"Excuse me," he says, in this scared little voice—

making out like he's me and I'm standing on a stage in a club, scared and shy and trying to get the attention of a noisy crowd.

"Excuse me," he says. "Hello . . . Can I have your attention . . . ? Would you mind, if . . . ?

"Hello . . . ? Would anybody out there like to hear a song . . . ? A short song . . . ?

"Yes . . . ? No . . . ? Okay . . . Well, then . . . I'll just start . . . And if I get too loud or anything, just . . .

"Okay, then . . . A-one . . . A-two . . . Oh, never mind . . . Sorry . . . Excuse me . . . I . . ."

And apologizing and ducking his head, like he's slinking off the stage that he's been standing on, he starts backing away from me.

And even though I hate to give him the satisfaction, I can't help it, the picture he's painted is so pathetic, I just break out laughing.

"Okay," I tell him. "What do I have to do?"

"Make me want you," he says.

The way he's looking at me, I can't tell if—

"You're kidding," I guess.

"No," he says.

He's not kidding!

"You want me to make you want me?!" I ask him.

"Yes," he says.

"How am I supposed to do that?" I ask him.

"By pretending that you want me," he suggests.

"Pretending . . . ?"

"Play," he says.

"The same song?"

He nods.

"But slower," he says. "Kind of lazy . . . Yeah, like that."

I'm strumming away at about half the tempo I was strumming before.

"And don't sing until I tell you," he says, "okay?"

"Okay."

79

"Now, just for the hell of it, try to imagine that you're the girl in the song, the girl that you're singing about, the girl who's—"

"Hot to trot?"

He nods.

"So hot!" he says. "This place that you're in, this juke joint on the edge of a piney woods just outside of New Orleans, it's sweltering. There's no air-conditioning. No fans even. And no breeze to speak of.

"The closest thing to cool is the beer bottle that the waiter sets down on your table. And it's sweating, too. You can feel it.

"As you press the cool bottle to your chest, you can feel the beads of perspiration trickling down between your breasts. Ahh!

"You close your eyes, and when you open them, he's looking at you—the most amazing-looking guy.

"Not me," he says, "but somebody—anybody that you ever dreamed of really getting it on with."

I think about Donnie Pelligrino.

"Or better yet," he says, "if you ever really got it on with somebody so hot that you can't wait to get it on with him again, imagine him."

Since nobody in that particular category leaps to mind, I stick with Donnie—trying to picture him in this place, this juke joint outside of New Orleans on this sweltering hot day.

"He's not alone," says Jasper. "A guy like that, he wouldn't be alone.

"And the woman he's with—the women! Two of them. One hotter looking than the next and the two of them together—Look out!"

I can see them, all right. But Donnie—it's almost impossible to even picture him in my mind with this guy, Jasper, standing right here in front of me, as big as life.

"If you're thinking about walking out of here with this guy, you're gonna have to show him something, Holly.

Like how much you want him. More than both of those beautiful girls together. So much, you won't let anybody come between you. So much, you won't let anything stand in your way.

"Show him, Holly. Tell him all about it . . ."

> *"Some girls, they stop at nothing.*
> *They give you all they got . . ."*

Like I'm that girl, that kind of girl, I sing it low and slow.

> *"And other girls, they ask you 'Why?'*
> *But this girls says, 'Why not?'*
> *So . . ."*

"A little faster, now . . ."

> *"It's no wonder, since she came,*
> *Everybody knows her name.*
> *Once she's started, she can't—"*

Oh, boy!
"What's wrong?"
I've stopped singing.
"Are you all right?"
I can't tell Jasper why.
"You were doing okay," he says.
I can't tell him how, just a moment ago in the juke joint, he pushed his chair back from the table that he was sitting at.
And how, after excusing himself to the two beautiful women that he was sitting with, he smiled over at me, like he was sealing the deal, and got to his feet.
"I was thinking," he says, "maybe, if we really threw ourselves into it, heart and soul, morning, noon, and night

from now straight through to the end, and if the competition was weak enough . . .''

I can't tell Jasper how it felt—how I felt—when I imagined him walking across the floor of the juke joint, coming to get me and take me away with him because—*I don't want to think about it!*

"Wanna dance?" he asks me.

"Now?!" I ask him.

He grins and shakes his head.

"No," he says. "Monday night at the Cobblestone."

"Oh," I say, like I'm used to accepting invitations from ghosts, like I do it all the time. "Sure."

TWENTY

''This is fun, hon. But if I don't get a fresh fanny in this chair, quick as a flash, Jenette is going to have a cow!''

For the last fifteen minutes, my old pal Jon, who cuts my hair when I get it cut, has been showing me how I'd look if I wore my hair in an upsweep or a French knot or in a thick braid or a ponytail.

But now, with his boss, the bovine Jenette, eyeing him from her perch behind the cash register, he's getting a little nervous.

"Of course," he whispers, "it takes one to have one, but still—"

I laugh and check myself out in the mirror.

"This is good!" I tell him.

"This?!" he says. "This is what you came in with, only a little shorter!"

"And better shaped!"

"Yes," he says, "but I thought we were out to impress somebody special!"

"We are!" I tell him. "Me!"

"Oh!" he says. "Self-improvement! I like that!"

It's true, too, what I've told Jon.

It wasn't because I wanted to impress Jasper that I decided at the last minute to get my hair cut.

I was due. It's been months. Weeks, anyway.

On the other hand, I don't mind if Jasper finds me looking a little better than what he's used to when he meets me at the Cobblestone tonight.

I mean, he's never once seen me looking like anything but my usual everyday ordinary self and if, after seeing me like that, he thinks that I have even an outside chance of winning this thing, then maybe, if I look a little better than that, he'll think that I've got a little better chance of winning.

And if Jasper feels better about my chances, then I probably will too.

And I've already noticed, when I feel better about my chances, I also feel better about myself and just better in general.

So, it's really for me that I decided, after work today, I'd get my hair done for tonight.

That's also the reason that I decide, when I walk out of Jenette's and see that Murphey's, the department store on the other side of the mall is still open—that's why I decide that I might as well pick up a lipstick to replace the cherry red one that I told Jasper about and which it seems that I've lost.

And it's only because there's practically nobody in the store and nobody at all at the cosmetics counter that I take a second while I'm at it to check out a couple other shades of lipstick.

"Try the russet," says the saleslady. "This one. Not everyone can wear it, but with your coloring . . ."

I put a little on the back of my hand, hold it up by my face and look into the mirror.

"Yeah," I say. "I see what you mean."

She's got a great eye this lady and, because she does, and because she's so nice and takes so much time with me, I let her sell me a complimentary shade of eyeliner and, because it's on a special offer, some blusher, too.

And then, when she's finished ringing up the sale and I've finished wringing most of the cash out of my wallet, she says, "Thank you," and I say, "Thank you," and "Oh!" like I just remembered, "What floor is lingerie . . . ?"

TWENTY-ONE

"Hey!" says Stuey Ahrens.

"Hey yourself!" I tell him.

I'm on the dance floor, dancing with myself, which I don't mind since the dance floor at the Cobblestone is always so crowded, whoever you start out dancing with, you always wind up dancing with yourself anyway.

Stuey, who was just passing by when he noticed me, wedges his way onto the floor and into a spot opposite me.

"You alone?" he says.

"Kind of," I tell him.

Jasper hasn't shown up yet. At least, not that I know of.

"I'm working," he says.

"Yeah," I tell him, "I know."

"If I wasn't, though . . ." he says.

"Yeah?" I ask him.

He shrugs. "You look different," he says.

"Thank you?"

He smiles. "Better," he says.

"Good?" I ask him.

"Yeah," he says.

"Flatterer!"

He laughs.

So do I.

"Well . . ." he says.

"You've got to go," I guess.

"Yeah," he says. "See you."

"Yeah," I say. "Hey!"

"Huh?"

"Do you know any girls that'd be interested in joining my band?"

"Your band?" he asks me.

I wonder why I said "girls." I guess it's because that's what I meant. Although, up until now, I hadn't really thought about it, but—

"Yeah," I tell him. "I'm putting a band together and entering it in the Playoffs."

I wait to see how he reacts to that.

But he doesn't. He thinks for a second and then, he shakes his head and tells me, "Not right off, no."

"Will you think about it?" I ask him.

"Me?!" he says.

I laugh and shake my head. "About if there are any girls," I tell him.

"Oh, yeah!" he says. "Sure."

"Thanks," I tell him.

"Any time," he says. "Well . . ."

"Later," I tell him.

"Yeah," he says.

And he wedges his way back off the dance floor.

"You should see the stuff they've got back there!" says Jasper, materializing in front of me.

I'm so used to his doing that by now, I don't freak out, like any normal person would.

I just smile with my russet red lips and toss my silken hair and say, "Hi!"

And right away, some guy that I've never seen before, but who happens to be looking my way, smiles back at me and says, "Hi!" like I'm talking to him, instead of to my invisible dancing partner.

I turn away from the guy.

And Jasper, imitating the moves of one of the slicker dancers on the floor, a blond bombshell in a skirt no wider than my belt, moon dances over to a spot in front of me.

"Not bad," I tell him.

"If you like cheap blondes," he says, "like I do."

Before I can tell him that it was his dancing I was complimenting and not his cheap blonde, he nods to the space behind the bandstand where the bands stack their gear, and he says, "They've got more stuff back there—these kids, these amateurs—then The Who had when they played the Garden back in Sixty-Six!"

I try it again. I toss my silken hair and part my russet red lips and say, "Hi."

"Hi," he says. "It's incredible, the power they've got, the control!"

"Yeah," I say.

"I want to go check out the room," he says, "the sound balance and sight lines, before the show starts. Where do the judges sit for the Showdown?"

"Over there," I tell him, nodding toward the table at the side of the bandstand, where Arthur sits with the record business guys who he gets down from New York City to help him pick the winner of the Showdown.

"Do you mind?" he asks me, and, like he can't imagine why I would, he adds, "Thanks," and—*phhtt!*—he's gone.

" 'Do you mind?' " I mutter, loud enough for the girl

who just backed into me to say, "Sorry!" and shoot me a dirty look, like it was *me* that backed into *her*.

"Okay, who is he?" says Claudia, as I walk off the dance floor, a couple minutes later.

For a second, I'm afraid she's caught sight of Jasper. I know that's crazy, but—

"Who's who?" I ask her.

She gives me this look, like *"Who do I think I'm kidding?"*

"The guy you're turned out for," she says.

"I can see your bra," says Eddie, staring bug-eyed at the black lace bra that I picked up at Murphey's.

I'm wearing it under Bryan's old work shirt, which I'm wearing unbuttoned, like a jacket, over my tightest-fitting jeans.

"You're supposed to," Claudia tells him.

"Oh," says Eddie like, if he's supposed to, then why bother? And then, nodding toward the men's room, he tells Claudia, "I'm gonna . . ."

"If you gotta, you gotta," says Claudia.

"I gotta," Eddie tells her and then, turning to me before he goes, he says, "Nice bra."

"Thanks," I tell him.

"But," he says, "your hooters, man . . ."

And he shakes his head and waggles his hand, like so-so, and cracks himself up.

And then, shrugging off my killer glare like it was nothing, he turns around and walks away.

"What a dick!" says Claudia.

But from the way that she says it and the smile on her face as she watches him go, you can see, whatever she says, she's nuts about the guy.

"What else is new?!" I say.

She turns to me and looks me over. "You tell me!" she says. "Come on! There's got to be a guy!"

"There isn't!" I tell her.

87

"Then you must be on the prowl for one," she says.

"Why does it have to be a guy?" I ask her. "Just because I feel like getting dressed up for a change, why does it have to be for some guy? Especially since, off hand, I can't think of one of them that isn't as big a dick as Eddie is?"

"Well, you don't have to get mad about it!" says Claudia.

"It *makes* me mad," I tell her, "the way some people think that everything a girl does, she does just to get on the good side of some . . ."

"Dick?" she guesses.

"Yeah," I say.

She laughs and, like she still doesn't believe me, she says, "Okay. So if it isn't a guy that you're dressed up for, what is it?"

"I'm celebrating," I tell her.

She looks at me. "Am I supposed to guess why?" she asks me.

I shake my head. I don't know how to do this, where to begin.

"Do you know how I've been telling you that you should join up with a band?" I ask her.

"Yeah . . ." she says.

"Well," I tell her, "I've decided to take my own advice."

She looks at me like I'm cracked, but I go on.

"So how would you feel about joining my band?" I ask her.

"Your band . . . ?" she says.

"Yeah," I say. "What would you say, if I told you it was going to be just girls in it? And we were going to get into the Playoffs? And kick ass? And win? And go on to the Showdown? And kick ass again? And win that, too? What would you say?"

"What are you on?" she says.

"Huh?"

"Are you on drugs?"

I laugh, but—

"I'm serious," I tell her.

She looks at me, hard, looks into my eyes and shakes her head and, like she can't believe it, she says, "You are, aren't you?"

"I know it sounds crazy," I say.

"It *is* crazy," she tells me.

"I don't think so," I tell her.

But the look she gives me—

"Okay," I concede. "Maybe, it is, but—so what? What have we got to lose? I mean, after all, what does anybody expect of us, anyway? Except for us to be there when they want us? And do whatever it is that they want us to do?

"So what's the big deal, if we try to do what we want to do for a change? What's the big deal, if it doesn't work out? Which I happen to think that it will."

"It won't," she says, like she's dead certain.

"You don't know," I tell her.

"I do!" she insists. "Believe me, Holls. If you think you can just throw together an all-girl band with me and you and God knows who and go into the Playoffs and beat out bands as good as Bent and the rest of them . . ." She shakes her head. "You're crazy, Holls, whacko. I'm sorry, but you just are."

"I know you think that," I tell her.

"I like your voice," she says. "I've always said it and meant it and I still do, but . . ."

She looks me in the eye and, shaking her head like she pities me, like I'm a hopeless case, she says, "Good golly, Miss Holly!"

I want to tell her about my secret weapon, about Jasper. I'm dying to tell somebody about him.

But I know, even though she's my best friend, if I told

her, "There's this ghost that I know . . ." she'd either laugh in my face or phone for the folks from the funny farm, so—

"I had a dream," I tell her.

She looks at me.

"There was this guy in the dream, this rock 'n' roll star—"

"Holly!"

"He promised he'd teach me—!"

"Yo! Holls! Listen! My pop, Izzy, you know how much money he's lost on dream numbers that don't hit and dream horses that don't come in?"

"This isn't like that," I tell her.

"And anyway," she asks me, "what do I need to be a musician for? Isn't it enough I got Izzy and Eddie? And now, you?

"I mean, who's gonna' stay home and take care of the house and kids?" she asks me. "Who's going to hold down a job, while all you guys are out there hustling your butts, trying to get some hot record company guys to make stars out of you and work you to death and steal you blind?"

"I'm serious," I tell her. "We can win this thing."

She shakes her head.

"You're dreaming," she says.

"If it's Eddie that you're worried about . . ." I tell her.

"Yeah . . . ?"

I've just noticed him. He's out on the dance floor, dancing with—

"Who is that?" Claudia asks me.

She's followed my gaze to the dance floor, to Eddie and the girl that he's dancing with, the blonde bombshell, the one that Jasper—

"I don't know," I tell her.

"Son of a bitch!" she says.

And she sets out for the dance floor.

"Wow!" says Jasper.

"You again!" I say.

"Who is she?"

"I don't know."

"You called her Claudia."

"Oh," I say, "her."

"She's fantastic!"

"Yeah," I say, "great hooters."

"Huh?"

"And she's a terrific drummer, too."

"Really!"

"You wanna dance?"

"Huh?"

"You said, 'Let's go dancing.' Remember?"

"Oh!" he says. "Yeah. Sure."

"Leslie Lee and the Leroys!" shouts Arthur Kilburn, bounding out onto the bandstand. "Let's hear it for them! Leslie Lee! The Leroys!"

"Sorry," says Jasper.

"It's Monday night! Amateur Night! And time for the Cobblestone's world famous Amateur Night Playoffs!"

"Yeah," I tell him, "me, too. Very."

TWENTY-TWO

I can't tell you what it was in particular, why I told Jasper that I was going to the ladies' and excused myself and got up from the table where we were sitting and just walked out the door and kept right on walking.

It wasn't how good the first two bands were. Although

Moon Pie, who came all the way from Akron, Ohio, where Chrissie Hynde comes from, was pretty good. And Slurp, being hairless and snarling, was pretty funny. And they did make me wonder if Claudia wasn't right about my being nuts to think, with so little time to go before the Showdown, I could put together an all-girl band that could blow the competition off the Cobblestone stage.

But it wasn't just how good the bands were tonight that put me in the pits and shot me out the door.

No. It was my best friend, Claudia, looking me in the eye and telling me that what I wanted to do was impossible because she was afraid that she didn't have the nerve even to help me try.

I guess that it's getting into a contest with her boyfriend, Eddie the "hooter" man that she's afraid of. Like *"What if I beat him?"*

But how about it's *him* that's beaten *her?* Beaten her out of living her own life? Beaten her down so far she doesn't dare make a move on her own?

Otherwise, I know she'd love to be playing in a band. She would! I know because I've seen how happy she is when she's just down in her basement, playing for nobody but herself and me. And even when she's just talking about times that she's played with Izzy, her pop, and the guys that he plays with, or the time at the rehearsal with Bent, she just lights up.

So why, when I asked her to play in my band, if it wasn't that she was worrying about how Eddie would take it, why would she tell me that what I'm trying to do is impossible?

When all it is, really, is extremely unlikely?

And so what if it is?

Unless Claudia knows something that I don't know, the only thing that would make it impossible for us to win the Showdown would be if we didn't enter the Playoffs.

Which—thanks to Claudia—is probably what I'll wind up doing, since without her I've got nothing.

Except for this stupid bra that I'll probably burn, as soon as I get home.

And a lot of egg on my face, for getting myself all worked up about something as extremely unlikely as—

Except, now that I think about it, it wasn't me who got me dressed up and hyped up like this, was it?

I mean, I didn't fill my own head with impossible dreams, did I?

No, it wasn't.

And no, I didn't.

No, the jerk that put me up to all this was—

"I'm sorry!" says Jasper, falling into step beside me. "I thought everybody had indoor plumbing these days. Is this the way to the outhouse?"

"Yes," I tell him. "You take a left up here at Fleet Street and walk straight into the ocean."

"Ah!" he says. "So you're the one that's responsible for killing all the fish!"

"Yes," I say, "and you're the one that's responsible for feeding me a load of—"

"Exceptional opportunities?" he says. "Yes, I am. Did you hear those clowns, tonight?"

"Clowns?!" I ask him. "You mean Moon Pie?!"

"Oh," he says. "They were all right."

"Slurp, then? Is that who you mean?"

"No," he says. "I wouldn't call them clowns, either. Convicts, maybe, but—"

"So, who are you talking about, then?" I ask him.

"The winners," he says.

I look at him.

"Johnny Reb," he says. "Four of the prettiest guys with the most beautiful hair you've ever seen."

"You're kidding!"

"Well," he says, "three of them were pretty. One of them was only very handsome."

"What did they play?"

He shrugs. "They looked like guitars," he says, "but they sounded like tortured dogs."

I break up. "It isn't funny," I tell him.

"I called the ASPCA," he says.

"Claudia turned me down!"

"Bummer!" he says.

"Tell me about it!" I say.

"Was this before the fight?" he asks me. "Or after?"

"Fight?"

"Claudia and—what was his name? You know, 'Duh . . .' "

"Eddie."

"Yes."

"What happened?"

Jasper shrugs. "Something about a bimbo," he says.

"Yeah?"

"That's what she was shouting—"

"Claudia?"

"—as she went out the door," he says. "Yes."

"And Eddie?"

"He was shouting, 'Wait up!' as he went out after her," he says. "But the way it looked, she wasn't listening."

"Really?"

"Have you ever known a ghost to lie?"

"Have I?" I ask him. I look him in the eye.

He smiles at me and puts his hand over his heart and says, "Never!"

I nod, wanting to believe him, wanting to believe that, maybe, this dream that he sold me can still come true and wondering if Claudia might yet be a part of it, or if her fight with Eddie was just another of their lovers' quarrels that always end up with them getting back together again, even closer than they were before.

And that's where I am, off someplace between wanting and wondering, when Jasper says, "I like your hair that way."

"Huh?" I say.

Not because I didn't hear him, but because he just got through telling me that he never lies, and here he is—

"It looks good," he says.

I look at him and tell him, "Thanks."

"The way it moves when you walk," he says. "So light and airy."

"Thank you."

"Except—"

Ah!

"Except . . . ?" I ask him.

"The way you walk," he says.

I stop walking.

He does, too.

"What's wrong with the way I walk?"

"You trudge," he tells me.

"Trudge?"

He nods. "Like a soldier with a full backpack," he says.

"When I should—what?" I ask him. "Float like a water rat?"

He laughs and shakes his head.

"How does a star get onto a stage?" he asks me.

I take a wild guess. "He walks?"

"Right," he says. "And how he walks out on stage, that first impression he gives the crowd in the very first moment that they set eyes on him, that sets the tone for everything that follows."

"If I trudge, then I'm a drudge?"

"Like that," he says. "A star struts out onto a stage— or into a room, for that matter—like it belongs to him, like he owns it."

"Like . . . ?" I ask him.

He smiles and, like a headwaiter, bowing and gesturing me to my table, he bends from the waist, motions me forward and says, "Please."

I ask myself, *"Do I have to put up with this?"*

I answer myself, *"Do you want to be a rock 'n' roll star?"*

95

I smile to myself and, nodding to Jasper, I say, "Thank you."

And I start walking.

Jasper does, too.

He catches up with me and walks along beside me.

And after a while, as we walk along Moore Avenue, headed toward my house, moving past sleeping houses, through scattered pools of lamplight, he says, "As you walk, think about what you're doing. See yourself walking . . .

"Feel your body moving through the air. Feel it moving inside your clothes. Feel your clothes moving against your skin . . .

"Relax," he says. "Relax everything. Surrender every muscle, head to toe. Surrender to the gentle pull of gravity . . .

"Feel the earth beneath your feet. Feel your weight settling onto your feet, carrying you forward over the earth, pushing you through the air . . .

"That's it. Loose as a goose. Every joint ajangle. Like a fluid druid . . .

"Good. That's good . . .

"Now, notice how you're walking in time with your breathing in and your breathing out . . .

"That's what it's all about . . .

"Check it out!

"Feel the beat of your feet on the street . . .

"Now, you're walking to the rhythm of Holly's drum.

"Here we come . . .

> *"B'deep!*
> *Pow! Pow! Pow!*
> *Walkin' down the street*
>
> *B'deep!*
> *Pow! Pow! Pow!*
> *Boppin' to the beat*
> *Of Holly's drum.*

B'deep!
Pow! Pow! Pow!
Life can be so sweet.

B'deep!
Pow! Pow! Pow!
Now—
   Add a little
   Paradiddle—
            Holly's drum . . ."

It's like in a dream. One minute, we're walking down the street, and the next minute, we're up in Bryan's room dancing like a couple of rockers, wailing on our guitars and wearing out the floor.

   "B'deep!
   Pow! Pow! Pow!"

We've got all the furniture piled up in one corner and we've rolled back the rug.

And now, with Jasper twanging on his air guitar and me banging away on Bryan's old Gibson, he's showing me the moves and I'm trying to keep up with him.

   "B'deep!
   Pow! Pow! Pow!"

We're doing jumps and knee-drops, slides and kip-ups. *Okay! Jasper does the kip-ups, but—*
We're trying out cartwheels and back-to-backs and whirlybirds and—
"Duckwalk!" he shouts and—squatting and strutting and strumming, all at the same time—he boogies across floor.

It looks impossible, but—
Here I come . . .

> *"B'deep!*
> *Pow! Pow! Pow!*
> *Turnin' up the heat.*
>
> *B'deep!*
> *Pow! Pow! Pow!*
> *Wow—*
> > *Never slacken.*
> > *Let's get quackin'—"*

"Whoops!"
As I tip over and go sprawling across the floor, Jasper finishes without me.

> *"Holly's drum!"*

Too embarrassed to fight it, I surrender what's left of my pride. Lying on my back, I look up at the ceiling and let myself dissolve in a fit of helpless laughter.

But then, the next thing I know, Jasper's standing over me, looking down at me, his eyes diamond bright, a warm smile spreading across his face.

"Hot stuff!" he says, like it's me that he's talking about.

And maybe I'm stupid, but for just that second and for maybe the first time in my life, I believe it.

And the very next second, because it scares me so— believing it, imagining that he believes it—and because I can't think what to say, I laugh some more.

TWENTY-THREE

"**H**e said he was just dancing with her, you know? Marilyn. She must be thirty, to look at her. 'Just dancing . . .'

"But, 'Okay,' I told him. 'But at least you could of told me!'

" 'How am I supposed to tell you I'm dancing with her, when I'm *dancing* with her? Shout?' he says. 'Hey! Yo! Claudia! I'm dancing with Marilyn, here!'

" 'Marilyn . . .' " Claudia shakes her head. Behind her sunglasses, she's crying.

Laird—sitting at the counter next to her—gives her shoulder a squeeze.

"So you let it go?" I ask her.

"Yes, I let it go!" she says. "He's only dancing, right?"

"Right?" I ask her.

"Wrong," says Laird.

"If he's only dancing," says Claudia, "then how come he's got her phone number here?" Claudia shows me the palm of her left hand.

"I notice it during the show," she says. "I go to, you know, hold his hand. Like I forgive him, you know? And— 'What's this?!'

" 'Oh,' he says. 'A guy wants to sell his car. Speedo's looking for one like he's got, the guy. So . . .'

" 'So you wrote his number down on your hand?' I ask him.

" 'I didn't have no paper,' he says."

Claudia shakes her head.

" 'No paper . . . ', " she says. "The way he talks . . . 'Prick!' I call him. Loud enough for everybody to hear. And I get up to go."

" 'What?!' he says."

" 'Since when do you cross your sevens, like that?!' I ask him. 'Since you been living in Europe?!'

" 'Hey!' he says."

" 'Prick!' I call him, again."

" 'Wait up!' he says."

Claudia shakes her head, again.

"Fat chance!" she says.

"How'd you get home?" I ask her.

"Eddie drove me," she says.

"You let him?!"

She nods.

I shake my head.

"I can't believe you'd—"

"Pick up!" Carl calls to me from behind the grill.

"Be right back," I tell Claudia.

"Sorry," I tell Carl, as I pick up Helen Vogel's BLT down and a side of French. It's lunch hour at Avery's, toward the end of it, thank goodness, or I'd never be able to get away with spending so much time with Claudia.

"Your friend all right?" Carl asks me.

"Not yet," I tell him.

"Pretty girl," he says.

"That doesn't help," I tell him.

Before he can say anything to that, I grab my order and I'm gone.

"BLT down with a side of French!"

I put Helen Vogel's order down in front of her and ask her if there's anything else I can get her. She glances over at Claudia, shakes her head, and waves me away.

"Did he apologize, at least?" I pick up the conversation where I left off.

"Eddie?!" says Claudia. "He doesn't know the meaning of the word."

"Then—?"

"He said it wasn't my business who he danced with or fooled around with either. 'Fooled around' is what he said.

" 'Fooled around.' He sleeps with some bimbo, like Marilyn or some of these other ones that are still getting into the movies on kids' tickets, and he thinks it's fooling around.

"So I say, 'Right. What you do isn't my business, but what I do, who I see, that's your business, right?'

" 'Yeah,' he says. 'It's different what you do and what I do. You're a girl, a schoolgirl. I'm a musician, a rocker,' he says. 'I'm with a band!' he says.

" 'Yeah?' I tell him. 'Well, so am I!' "

Wha . . . ?!

" 'Since when?' he says.

" 'Since now,' I tell him.''

I'm holding my breath, afraid to believe what I'm hearing.

"And you know what he did?" Claudia asks me.

I shake my head.

"He laughed at her," says Laird.

"He laughed at me," says Claudia. "And when I told him whose band it was that I was in? That it was yours?"

"It *is*?!" I can barely contain myself.

Claudia nods. "If you've still got a spot for me," she says.

"If I've . . . ?"

"He laughed at *you,*" says Laird.

"Screw him!" I say.

"Yeah," say Claudia. "And the horse he rode in on!"

"Screw 'em all!" shouts Laird.

"Rock 'n' roll!" I shout.

I dive over the counter and wrap my arms—one of them around Claudia and one of them around Laird.

"Rock 'n' roll!" shouts Claudia.

And Laird.

And Carl.

And Helen Vogel.
And Alice shouts, "Easy listening!"

TWENTY-FOUR

I'm hot, hot, hot.

So is everybody else on the Jersey shore.

All through July and into August, it's been so hot and humid, if it wasn't for the lifeguards all looking off in the same direction, it'd be hard to tell the difference between the ocean and the shore.

But as hot as everybody else has been, I've been even hotter. Especially this last week, when every night, while Pop has been off, overseeing the annual Tourist Fleecing Contest, I've been up in Bryan's room, rehearsing with Jasper—singing my heart out, playing my fingers bloody, and dancing my ass off—getting ready for my first rehearsal with Claudia.

I mean, Claudia's really good. I'm not kidding about that.

And, at least until Jasper started working with me, I wouldn't have dared to play with her. But now—

"What do you think?" I ask Jasper.

I've just finished running through "Honky Tonk Woman" for him for the ten thousandth time.

It and "Jumpin' Jack Flash" are what we've been practicing with until I can come up with an original song of my own—something so terrific that, no matter how badly I perform it, people will just eat it up (and me along with it).

According to Jasper, coming up with a song like that

would give me my best shot at making my way past the Playoffs and coming out on top at the Showdown.

So, I promised him I'd try to come up with something, and he promised me that he'd help me bang it into shape if I did.

But so far, I haven't come up with anything worth talking about, let alone singing, so—

"That bad?" I ask him.

He's shaking his head. "Not bad for a girl," he says.

My goal, he's told me, should be to "play like a man, a big, bad man!"

"Great!" I say—meaning just the opposite, which Jasper knows by now.

"You're sweating like a man, though," he says. "That's progress."

"Maybe I should change before—"

"Is anybody home?"

A voice calls from downstairs.

"Claudia!" I tell Jasper.

"Be still my heart!" he says.

"Be still your mouth!" I tell him.

"Up here!" I shout.

And then, it hits me—

I'm not ready!

"I'm not ready, am I?"

Halfway to the door, I stop and turn back to Jasper.

"When she hears me bellowing and twanging and clumping around, she's going to turn around and walk out the door and never talk to me again.

"Except every time she passes me on the street, she'll bust out laughing and whisper to her new best friend and tell her how horrid I was, won't she?"

He laughs and says, "Wait till she sees the new, hard-body you."

"Oh! Yeah!" I say, like I forgot, which I did. With the way that Jasper's been working me out, I'm actually starting to show a little serious definition, here and there.

"Where are you at?"

Claudia calls again, this time from the second floor.

"Up here!" I call back to her.

"You can only be as good as you are," Jasper tells me.

"I'll try to remember that," I tell him, as I head for the door. "And you—you'll try to remember to keep your comments to yourself until Claudia's left?"

"Silent as the grave," he promises.

"You don't have to get morbid about it," I tell him, as I walk out onto the landing and look down the stairs.

"I should have learned to play the piccolo," says Claudia.

She's at the foot of the stairs and she's not alone. She's got a whole set of drums with her, packed in big black boxes, and a guy—like a native bearer—helping her with them.

"Hi, Stuey!"

"Hi, Holly," he says. "Is that it? The top of the mountain?"

"This is it," I tell him. "You want a hand?"

"No," he says. "That's okay."

Arriving at the top of the stairs, Claudia heaves a sigh, walks across the landing, and steps into our "rehearsal studio."

"This was Bryan's room?" she says.

"Yeah," I tell her, "before the hurricane hit."

"Looks like my room," says Stuey, schlepping a pair of drum cases through the door, "except for the cat."

"What cat?" says Claudia, looking around the room.

"My cat," says Stuey. "Where do you want these things set up?"

Claudia picks a spot by the window and Stuey gets to work, unpacking the drums and cymbals from their cases and getting them set up.

I didn't know Claudia had any drums like these. I knew that she had congas and bongos and gourds and stuff, but not regular drums like these and cymbals.

"Where'd you get the drums?" I ask her.

"Oh," she says. "I borrowed them."

"Ah!" I say, like that answers my question.

"There's a lot of stuff around," says Stuey. "Like if you need an electric guitar or anything. There's always a bunch of them floating around.

"You know how it is with musicians," he says. "Something new comes along, and, suddenly, nobody's happy with what they've got. Like, they're fickle, you know?"

I look at Claudia.

She looks at me.

Stuey looks up from the drums. "Did I say something?" he asks.

"A mouthful," I tell him. "But, yeah, if you could find me an electric guitar somewhere . . ."

"I'll ask around," he says.

"Thanks," I tell him.

"I've been thinking about people for your band, too," he says, "girls. But the only one that I've come up with, Jean Sifford, a bass player, I heard that she got pregnant and married and moved to Canada."

"Oh," I say, "well, thanks for thinking about it, anyway, but—do you mind if I ask you something?"

He shakes his head and says, "What do you want to know?"

I don't want to ask him, right out, why he's being so nice, like *"What's in it for you?"* I don't want to be rude or ungrateful or anything.

But on the other hand, I *am* curious, so—nodding to the drums that he's working on, that he hauled over here and lugged all the way up the stairs—I ask him, "Why?"

"Oh," he says. "Eddie asked me if I'd give Claudia a hand with them."

"They're Eddie's?!"

I look at Claudia.

She nods. "They're his old set," she says. "And since they were just sitting in his cellar, not doing anybody any good . . ."

"There you go!" says Stuey, finishing with the drums and standing back to admire his work.

"Hey," says Claudia, "thanks."

"Yeah," I say, "thanks a lot."

"Sure," he says, heading for the door and tossing a careless wave over his shoulder. "Good luck."

We stand there for a moment, Claudia and I, listening to Stuey thumping down the stairs, saying nothing until—finally—I have to ask her.

"So does this mean that Eddie doesn't mind if you play in my band anymore?" I ask her.

"Oh, he minds," she says. "It's just that he doesn't want to stand in the way of me making a fool of myself—which he says that I'm gonna because there's no way that we can put together any kind of a band around you singing lead."

"Do you believe him?" I ask her.

"I'm here," she says, like that answers it, which it does.

Smiling at her and hoping that she understands that I'm proud of her and grateful to her without my saying more, I nod and say, "Yeah."

"So," she says, "you want to play something?"

The moment of truth has arrived.

I take a deep breath and—

"Do you know 'Honky Tonk Woman'?" I ask her.

She laughs. "Takes one to know one," she says. "And if *I'm* not one . . ."

Without finishing, she just turns on her heels and struts on over to her drum set.

Settling down on her stool, she picks up her drumsticks and runs off a quick riff—kicking her bass, peppering her snare and tom-tom, bashing her cymbals until, after a second, when she's heard enough, she stops.

She makes a couple of minor adjustments—tightening a skin here, repositioning a cymbal there—and then, ready to roll, she lifts both drumsticks in the air, looks over at me, and gives me a nod.

"Okay," I tell her.

Here we go!

Under my breath, figuring he's somewhere nearby, I tell Jasper, "This better be good!"

"What?" says Claudia.

"Nothing," I tell her.

"Okay," she says.

I count off.

"A-one and . . ."

> *B'dee-bah-bah-bah*
> *Thump!*
> *B'dee-bah-bah-bah*
> *Thump!*

And the next thing you know, I've set sail for that bar room down in Memphis. And—*God!*—I can't tell you what it feels like, having that surge beneath you, that drive.

It lifts you up. It gives you such power—like a freight train rolling down a track, blowing its whistle, shouting, "Out of my way! Out of my way!"

It's great! And I don't care what anybody says, *we're great!* Claudia and I. We sound and look—and feel and taste and smell—*fabulous!*

"Rock n' roll!" Claudia bashes her cymbals one last time, tosses her drumsticks in the air, catches them, and finishes off the tune with *Rap, rap, rap* and a *Thump!*

"You think so?" I ask her.

I already know the answer, but I want to hear it again.

"Yes, I think so!" she says.

She runs a quick riff on her drum kit and shouts it again.

"Rock n' roll!"

And I shout it right back at her.

"Rock n' roll!"

She's smiling at me, like she's proud of me and like, between friends like us, it goes without saying.

"So what else do you know?" she asks me.

" 'Jumpin' Jack Flash'?"

"Do it!" she says.

We jump on it.

And when we're done, we go back to "Honky Tonk Woman."

Then "Jumpin' Jack Flash" again.

Until finally, when she can't stand it anymore, Claudia says, "If we're really going to do this—"

"We *are!*" I tell her.

"Yeah, well," she says, "then, we've got to get another song!"

"I know," I tell her.

"I don't mind losing," she says.

"*I* do!"

"But you go in there, playing a tune that everybody's heard a thousand times before and it's like *'Why bother?'* You know?"

"I know," I tell her.

"But if you could write something . . . ," she says.

"Yeah," I tell her. "I'm supposed to."

She looks at me.

Whoops!

"What do you mean, you're 'supposed to'?" she says.

Right!

"Nothing," I tell her. "Only that I promised myself that I would, but so far—nothing."

"But you're not gonna quit trying," she says.

"Never," I tell her.

"Okay, then," she says.

She puts down her drumsticks and, getting up from her stool, she steps out from behind her drum.

She spreads her legs wide and lifts her arms over her head and, graceful as a cat, she goes into this incredible undulating stretch that's so eye-popping—*she's* so eye-popping—I half expect to hear Jasper whistling or cheering or whispering some dark and dickly remark in my ear.

But, no, not a word from Jasper, not a sound.

For a second I wonder where he's got to.

But now, noticing that it's gotten late, Claudia asks me when we can get together again.

"Tomorrow?" I ask her.

"Sure," she says. "And what about the rest of us? What are you going to do about finding a couple of other players?"

"Yeah," I say, "a lead guitar or a keyboard player . . ."

"Even a bass would help," says Claudia.

"Yeah," I agree. "Damn that Jean Sifford! You'd think she'd be a little more careful, wouldn't you? In this day and age? A little more considerate of others?"

Claudia laughs. "You'd think," she says. "But what are you going to do?"

"Well," I tell her, "I've been thinking about putting up notices—on bulletin boards, bus stops. 'Musicians wanted. Call Holly Hanna at—' "

"Hello, Holly . . . ?" Dropping her voice down an octave, Claudia turns herself into a creep. "Whatcha doin', baby? You alone? Whatcha wearin'?"

I laugh and add, "Girls only!"

"So," she says, "what's stopping you?"

"Pop," I tell her. "There isn't much that gets past him."

"You haven't told him?"

I look at her, like *"Are you nuts?"*

"He's got to find out sometime."

"I know," I tell her.

"But you were hoping it wouldn't be until what? The second album?"

I laugh and tell her, "Okay. I'll get on it. Tomorrow. I promise."

She smiles. "Okay, then," she says. "Good night."

"Good night."

"It was, too," she says.

"Yeah," I tell her. "The best!"

As she turns around and heads for the door, I feel this little wave of satisfaction rising in my chest and—just as if Jasper was speaking my thoughts—I hear his voice in my ear, whispering, *"Not bad!"*

Without thinking, I tell him, "Thanks a lot."

"Thank *you!*" says Claudia.

At the door, she pauses and looks back at me.

"I meant Claudia," says Jasper.

"Oh," I say.

Claudia looks at me like I'm odd.

"The way she walks," says Jasper.

"Are you okay?" says Claudia.

"Oh!" I tell her. "Yeah! Why?"

"Oh, nothing," she says. "Only I don't remember you talking so much to yourself, like you've been doing, before."

"Oh, that!" I say. "I was just, uh, thinking. Out loud. Admiring, actually. The way that you walk."

"Oh!" she says. "Yeah. Like I'm a ring bearer, like at a wedding, and my ass is a velvet cushion that I'm bearing the jewel of my womanhood on."

"What?!" I shriek.

Claudia breaks up.

So does Jasper.

I shoot a dirty look in his direction.

"Estelle," says Claudia, citing the source of this gem.

"Who else?" I say.

"Only Estelle," she says. "Well . . ."

"Yeah," I say.

110

"See ya'," she says.

"Tomorrow," I say.

"But if you need to talk to somebody before then," she says, "you can always call me."

I look at her.

"Instead of talking to yourself," she says.

"Oh!" I say. "Yeah. Okay. Thanks. I will. Good night."

She says good night again and turns and struts across the room and carries the jewel of her womanhood out the door.

TWENTY-FIVE

"**H**i!"

The minute Claudia's out of sight, Jasper reappears.

"No more," I tell him.

"No more . . . ?" he says.

"Talking to me when she's around," I say.

"She can't hear me," he says.

"I know," I tell him. "It's *me* that she hears."

"Yeah," he agrees.

"Me, talking back to you," I tell him.

"Stop talking back," he suggests.

"I *will!*" I tell him. "If you stop *talking!*"

He doesn't say anything.

"Okay?" I ask him.

Nothing.

"Otherwise," I tell him, "somebody's going to catch

me at it and ship me off to where they pad the walls. So, okay?"

Still nothing.

He just stands there, looking at me, until finally I say, "Come on!" like *"Say something!"*

And he grins and tells me, "I was just practicing."

Like I'm not amused, I tell him, "Great! So . . . ?"

He heaves a sigh. "Okay," he says. "Even though it won't be as effective, I'll save all my comments and criticisms, good and bad—"

"Good?" I ask him.

He grins. "Not bad," he says.

"You're talking about the way we sounded?" I ask him. "And not about Claudia's walk?"

"Yeah . . .," he says.

"Is there a but?" I ask him.

"Other than Claudia's?" he says.

I laugh and tell him, "Yes!"

He nods and says, "Yes."

"Are you going to tell me what it is?"

"I've told you," he says.

"I didn't make you want me," I guess.

He shakes his head.

"I tried!" I tell him.

"I know," he says. "I could see you trying . . ."

"So," I ask him, "I looked—what? Slutty?"

He shakes his head.

"Silly?"

He doesn't answer.

Which is an answer.

"You know," he says, "with your hair like that, long, like you wanted to keep it . . ."

I can hear the frustration in his voice.

"Instead of just swishing it around and playing peekaboo with it, you could be *using* it—like Salome used her seven veils."

I look at him.

"You could be using it to tantalize all the guys sitting out front watching you, with little glimpses of the thing they most desire.

"With Salome," he says, "it was her body . . ."

"But you don't think that would work for me?" I guess.

He laughs, just like I thought he probably would, and he shakes his head.

"With you," he says, "it's—"

"My soul?" I say, like *You wouldn't try to kid me, would you?*

But like he isn't kidding, he nods and tells me, "Yes!"

So I laugh.

And I say, "Really!"

"Well," he says, thinking it over, "if not your soul itself, then—at least—the windows of your soul."

I think *that* over.

"You mean my eyes?" I ask him.

He doesn't answer.

Not directly or right away.

He's thinking, thinking back.

"There was this girl," he says. "I'll never forget her. Not fabulous to look at. I had lots of those. But—God!— this girl! I think she was British.

"When you looked in her eyes, just looked into her eyes, you could see her—or some part of her, as real as the girl who was standing there in front of you, reaching out to you, caressing your cheek, breathing softly in your ear, slipping her fingers inside your shirt, undoing your buttons, your belt, so tenderly, and giving herself to you, so entirely, so eagerly, so gratefully that later, when I thought back on the afternoon that we met and the night that we spent together, I couldn't separate the way that she imagined us together from the way that we actually were together. One experience was as real and as wonderful as the other. And now . . ."

"And now," I say, concluding his story with a moral

113

of my own, "you can't even remember what country she came from."

He smiles and admits it. "No," he says.

"Or what her name was?" I ask him.

"No," he says.

"Do you remember any of their names?"

"Sure," he says.

"And the faces that they go with?"

"Some," he says. "A few."

"But not hers?" I ask him.

"No," he says.

I want to ask him if he thinks that's why he's here—to meet a girl whose name he'll remember.

"But her eyes . . ." he says, smiling at the memory. "When I close my eyes, I can still see them."

And just for a second, I envy the girl whose eyes still shine in Jasper's memory.

"But that's as close as anybody ever got?" I ask him. "To touching your heart? As close as you got to loving anybody?"

Jasper laughs, and, like it explains everything, he says, "I was only twenty-one!" And then, quickly getting back to the subject, he adds, "But that's what I want your eyes to be like, like hers."

And I look into his eyes and I think, *"Me, too,"* but what I say is, "You mean, when I'm performing?"

"Yes," he says.

"Oh," I say, and as I nod and tell him, "No problem," I imagine myself reaching out to touch his cheek.

"Ow!"

I break up laughing.

"What is it?" he asks me.

"You need a shave," I tell him.

He looks at me, like I've lost my mind.

I haven't.

I think I just left it in my other pants.

TWENTY-SIX

It's been a long hot night.

Claudia and I have been up here in Bryan's room since right after dinner, auditioning the people who responded to the posters that I plastered around town. There's been six of them.

Jasper left after the third one, the accordion player who managed to get me and Claudia to play a back-beat version of "Lady of Spain." He couldn't take it anymore.

We couldn't either. But we had to. And so we did, from the time that Jasper took off around nine o'clock, until—well, it's almost eleven, now—through two lousy guitar players and a girl who played "Eleanor Rigby" on a clarinet that squeaked along with every note that she played, as if it was a Havahart trap with a frightened mouse caught inside it.

So now, when I ask Claudia, "Do you know what I hate?" it's no wonder that she guesses, "Music?"

"Yes," I tell her. "And life."

"Yeah," she says. "Me, too."

"I suppose, if we hadn't said 'Girls Only' . . ."

"Hello, Holly!" she says, in her deep-creep voice. "Remember me? Dick?"

I laugh and tell her, "Yeah, but . . ."

"Wait!" she says, raising a finger in the air and cocking her ear toward the door.

"Holly Hanna?"

A voice floats up the stairs.

"Should we hide?" I asked Claudia.

"Up here!" she shouts.

"Now you've done it!" I tell her.

I walk over to the door, tiptoe out onto the landing, and peek down the stairs.

Oh, boy!

The vision that greets me, the specter that I see climbing up the stairs, sends me scurrying back into Bryan's room where, in an urgent whisper, I announce the impending arrival of—

"Mary Ellen Vlasic!"

"No!" says, Claudia, as amazed—and alarmed—as I am.

Not that there's anything wrong with Mary Ellen Vlasic. Don't get me wrong.

It's just that Mary Ellen Vlasic is the tallest, skinniest, weirdest looking and oddest acting girl in my class at school—that's all. And what's she doing here?!

"Am I too late?"

"No!" I tell her, smiling a mile a minute.

She's standing on the landing, peeking in the doorway at us.

"Come on in," I say.

She looks at Claudia, like she's asking her permission.

"Yeah!" says Claudia. "How y' doing, Mary Ellen?"

"Hard to say," she says.

Ducking through the doorway—she must be at least six foot six—and stepping into the room, she holds up this carrying case that looks like it might hold a fishing rod or a pool cue or something other than a guitar.

"This is a bass," she says.

I look at Claudia.

"We can use a bass player," says Claudia. "Can't we, Holly?"

"Yeah," I say.

"Holly's the leader," she explains to Mary Ellen.

Mary Ellen doesn't look surprised.

That's how weird she is.

116

"Oh," she says.

"It was my idea," I explain, "forming a band. But I didn't know you played bass."

For years now, from grade school through high school, I've been going to assemblies, sitting in dimly lit auditoriums, and fidgeting in my seat while Mary Ellen Vlasic stood up on the stage, sawing away on her violin, playing some classical piece that I never heard of—playing really well, as far I could tell—but this is the first I've heard that she played the bass guitar.

"I don't," she says.

"Oh," I say—like *"I see!"*—which I don't.

"The guy where I rented it, you know Ken Woodward? He said of all the instruments in a standard rock 'n' roll ensemble, it was the easiest one to pick up. It's called a stick, this one, for the same reason I am, because of how it's . . ."

"Straight?" I guess.

"Yeah," she says, laughing. "I was looking for a word. Straight. That's us, yeah. Nice room. Like a teepee."

"Yes," I say, looking with new eyes at the slanting roof that forms the walls and ceiling of the room.

Mary Ellen sets down her carrying case, opens it, and pulls out this "stick" of hers—which is like a bass guitar that's all neck and no body.

The family resemblance is hard to miss.

"You can plug it in here," I tell her.

I show her the socket on the amp that Stuey got me, the one that came with the Stratocaster that he got me that he borrowed from a guy that he knew, who'd "gone acoustic" and—at least for the time being—had "no use for the juice."

Strapping the stick around her neck, Mary Ellen gets up to her feet, plugs in, and starts tuning up.

"Give me a second," she says.

"Sure," I tell her.

"We're not going anywhere," says Claudia.

117

I shoot her a look.

Now, hunched over her stick and pacing back and forth, so she looks like an enormous floating question mark, Mary Ellen starts getting acquainted with her new toy, picking its strings, fingering over its frets until—in what seems like no time at all—she's got this nifty little rhythm thing going.

> *B'doom, doom, doom, doom.*
> *Bip.*
> *Bop.*
> *B'doom, doom, doom, doom, doom.*
> *Bip!*

I look at Claudia.

She looks at me.

"Okay," says Mary Ellen. She stops playing.

"I'm ready for my audition," she says. "What do I do?"

"Do you know 'Honky Tonk Woman'?" I ask her.

"Not by name, no," she says, "but—"

"You've probably heard it," I tell her. "It goes like this."

I show her the chords.

"Oh, that!" she says.

> *B'dee-bah-bah-bah*
> *Thump!*
> *B'dee-bah-bah-bah*
> *Thump!*

And just like that, after hearing it once, she's got it down.

> *B'dee-bah-bah-bah*
> *Thump!*
> *B'dee-bah-bah-bah*
> *Thump!*

And now, with Claudia and me jumping in and riding along, Mary Ellen starts to groove on it and move to it.

And the next thing I know, she's got the tail of her shirt pulled out of her jeans and its buttons popped open from her neck to her navel and she's starting to work up a little sweat.

And now—*Look at her!*—like a white Manute Bol of rock 'n' roll, she's dancing, cutting loose, loose as a goose, into it, cookin', shakin' 'n' bakin'!

And me, too—me and Claudia—we're with her all the way, playing our hearts out and our asses off.

And then, I'm singing and soaring and letting the music take me where it will.

And where it takes me, well, there's this thing, this thing that's supposed to happen with great singers which—I don't have to tell you—I'm not.

But with really terrific singers like Bonnie Raitt, when they're really airing it out like I'm doing now, they get this thing called an overtone—like a second note or a ghost note—that comes from a sympathetic vibration of their vocal cords and makes it sound like they're singing two notes at once, with the overtone chiming in just a little over or under the main note they're singing.

The reason I mention this is, I've got it!

It's happening!

Now!

As I sing, I swear, I can hear this high-pitched overtone, squealing in my head and—*"God!"* I think. *"I'm doing it! I'm doing it!"*

Except it doesn't change, this note.

When my voice goes up and down, it just sticks to its guns.

Except, no, it gets louder—louder and louder until—

"Hold it!"

I stop playing.

Claudia stops a second later.

"What is it?" she asks me.

It's a second more before Mary Ellen's able to rein herself in.

"Listen," I say.

For a moment, the last notes we played hang suspended in the air and then, as they drop away off in the night, you can hear the high-pitched wail of a siren.

"Police," says Claudia.

"So?" says Mary Ellen.

"Her pop's a cop," says Claudia.

"Yeah . . . ?" says Mary Ellen, like *"So what?"*

But the siren is louder, now, like the police car that it's on is getting closer.

"Probably Pop forgot his glasses," I crack.

But nobody laughs.

I go to the window—it's open of course, the night being as hot as it is—and lean out and look down at the street and—*Jesus!*—it *is* Pop!

With its siren blasting and its red light flashing, Pop's police cruiser comes screeching to a stop, right in front of our house.

And now he's out the door and charging up the walk.

And now . . .

TWENTY-SEVEN

"**W**hat in the name of Jesus have you done with this room?"

That's the first thing Pop wants to know—what I've done to Bryan's room.

Amazed and enraged, he sweeps his eyes over our little stash of gear.

"And what is all this business that's got the whole neighborhood up in arms like they never were before, and ringing the phone down at the dispatcher's off the hook, like you'd think a bomb went off?" he wants to know. "And why aren't you kids—? I know you," he says to Claudia. "But who are you?"

Before he proofs Mary Ellen, I jump in and tell him, "She's my friend—"

"Some recommendation!" he says.

"—M—Mary Ellen Vlasic," I tell him.

Eyeing Mary Ellen, like he's trying to remember if, maybe, he didn't see her down by the school yard, pushing dope or something, Pop says, "I've seen you around."

"I'm hard to miss," she tells him.

"You're Don Vlasic's girl?" he asks her.

"*Vera*'s and Don's," she says.

"If you've got a home, then why aren't you there, this hour of the night," he asks her, "instead of hanging around my house with my delinquent daughter, disturbing the bejesus out of the peace?"

"Because we're rehearsing!" I tell him.

He doesn't even ask, "What for?"

"Out!" he tells Mary Ellen.

"You, too!" he tells Claudia.

He starts hustling my friends out of the room.

"They're my guests, Pop! I invited them!"

He warns them, if he ever catches them playing their "heavy metal music" around here again, he'll write up charges against them and "take custody of your instruments, pending disposition."

"You can't do that!" I tell him.

"He can't do that!" I shout to my friends, as they thump down the stairs.

"The hell I can't," he tells me.

"Sorry, Mary Ellen!" I shout.

"Quiet!" he tells me.

"Keep your eyes open," I shout to Claudia, "for someplace where we can rehearse in peace."

"I told you!" he warns me.

"Write a song!" Claudia shouts.

"Get a life!" shouts Mary Ellen—talking to Pop, I suppose.

I hear the front door slam.

And I turn to Pop.

I could kill him.

"These people," he tells me, "they've got a right to live, too, you know?"

He's talking about our neighbors, the Calderones, who called the cops on me.

"I know, Pop, but—"

"They've got rights," he says.

"Yes, but—"

"Including the right to vote," he says.

"I know, Pop—"

"And in this house," he says, "it's votes that keep the food on the table and the clothes on your back, and it's votes that will be sending you off to college one day.''

There he goes! Sending me off to college, again! You'd think he'd get it by now. Get it and let it go, but no!

"One day is about as long as I'd last," I remind him.

"Now, don't start that!" he warns me.

Like I started it! Like it isn't always him that starts it!

"I'm not college material!" I tell him for the two millionth time.

"Get to be!" he says.

"How?"

"Apply yourself!" he says.

"I have!" I tell him.

"Aah!" he says.

"I've tried!" I tell him.

"Try harder!" he says.

"That's not who I am!" I tell him.

"Oh?" he says. "Who are you, then?"

"If you have to ask . . ."

That gets to him.

"I'll tell you who you are," he says. "You're your mother's daughter. And you're going to go to college like I promised her you would."

"Because you promised her?" I ask him.

"Because I'm telling you!" he says.

"Because Mom didn't have any idea who I'd turn out to be, you know?"

"Oh," he says. "And I suppose you do!"

I nod. "I know who I am," I tell him.

Like he doesn't believe me, he says, "Oh?"

"Well," I admit, "maybe not exactly, but . . ."

"Ahh!" he says.

"But better than anybody else around here does," I tell him. "Except for Bryan. Except he's not around here anymore. But he's the only one who ever took the time."

"He's the only one who had the time!" he says.

"You make time for what you want to make time for," I tell him.

"Don't tell me what I do!" he warns me.

"Then don't you tell me what I do!" I tell him.

Raising his voice, he says, "So long as you live here—!"

"One year!" I tell him. "And then I'm gone!"

"Gone to college," he says.

I shake my head. "No way!"

He pays me no attention. "And there you'll stay," he says, "until you're finished!"

"I won't finish," I warn him. "I'll fail. I swear!"

"You do that!" he says.

"I will!"

"Disgrace yourself and your family," he says. "Cover yourself with ashes and set yourself adrift in the world. See how you like it!"

"I will!" I warn him. "I swear!"

"No, you won't!" he tells me.

He's shouting, now.

"You'll finish what you started," he says, "and then we'll see who you are and what you want to do with your life."

"I already know what I want to do with my life!" I insist.

"What?" he demands.

"Not go to college!" I shout.

And he gives me this look, like how did he wind up having such a fool for a daughter. And he shakes his head at his lousy luck. And he turns and starts for the door.

"Go to bed," he says.

"Go to hell!" I tell him.

It happens so fast, I don't think he even thinks about it. He just wheels around and in the same motion—*Crack!*— he slaps my face.

But so hard, for a second I see *stars!* And the sound of it—*Deafening!*—like a clap of thunder or a gunshot!

"You don't talk that way to your father," he says, his voice coming at me—all echoy, like from the bottom of well.

"Never!" he says.

He stands there, looking at me, waiting for me to say something or just cry.

But I won't give him the satisfaction.

I wait until he's gone and, even then, it's not until I wipe my mouth and see the streak of blood on the back of my hand and taste the blood in my mouth that I let go of my tears.

And, funny thing, as I drop to my knees and feel the first sobs wracking my body, I get this feeling that Jasper is back, not saying anything for now, but watching over me, standing by me, just in case.

And funnier still, as awful as I feel right now, the thing that keeps running through my mind is . . .

TWENTY-EIGHT

"I wanna be a rock 'n' roll star.
So tough, you never seen nobody tougher . . ."

I awaken to the bite of pain at the corner of my mouth where Pop's slap split my lip. Without opening my eyes, I bring the tip of my tongue to the spot.

Jasper says, "Good morning."

125

I open my eyes and see him sitting on my bed, which is really Bryan's mattress, which I've taken off his bed and set on the floor, so I can lean it up against the wall to make more room for Jasper and me to rehearse in.

I say, "Hi."

"How are you feeling?" he asks me.

"Sore," I tell him.

"Sore like in 'ow'?" he asks me. "Or sore like in 'grrr'?"

I grin, and it hurts, so I say, "Ow!" which makes me mad, so I say, "Grrr!"

And Jasper laughs.

"I hate him!"

Jasper nods and says, "Maybe."

"I do!" I tell him. "I hate my father!"

"You think he hates you?" he asks me.

"I don't care!" I insist. "What are you smiling about?"

"The look on your face when you said that."

"Like what?" I ask him.

"Like you cared," he says.

"Well, I don't!" I shout.

And it hurts when I shout, and I want to cry, but Jasper—goddamn him!—he's amused.

So I warn him, "Cut it out!"

And when he doesn't, I grab my pillow and swing it at him.

But, of course, it passes clean through him.

Which, of course, cracks him up.

So I call him, "Air head!"

And I jump out of bed.

And—*whoops!*—I'm naked!

And—*God!*—I'm embarrassed!

Which, of course, Jasper sees—along with everything else!

But like I couldn't care less, I just turn my back on him and stroll over to the closet, lift Bryan's work shirt from the doorknob, slip it on, and stroll over to the door that leads downstairs.

And of course Jasper never stops laughing the whole time.

So when I reach the door I tell him, "Kiss off!" and I moon him and—with his laughter echoing behind me—I march out the door.

I wanna hear 'em screaming when I play my guitar.
I wanna see the little boys suffer . . .

I go looking for Stuey Ahrens.

We need a place to rehearse, me and Claudia and Mary Ellen.

Yay! Mary Ellen! God! What a surprise! How great she played! How great she looked playing! And how great she made us sound—like with just one more of us, we might really be a band!

But we need to rehearse, and we need a place to do it, so, I'm looking for Stuey, because if anybody knows of a place for us to rehearse, it's him.

Only I'm not asking him about it or anything else until I find out what it is that he's after, why he's being so nice to us—helping Claudia with Eddie's drums and getting me a guitar and amp and everything.

I don't want Stuey thinking that I owe him anything that I'm not prepared to pay him back, you know?

Not that he is.

I don't know that he is.

The truth is, I don't know Stuey well enough to even guess what he's thinking. Up until I got into this rock thing, in my whole life I've hardly said anything more than "Hi" and "How's it going?" to Stuey.

And I never went out of my way to say that much.

After all, what do you expect? I mean, face it, Stuey's a year behind me at school and a couple of inches shorter than me and he's a roadie and—well, can you name one famous roadie?

So, anyway, I'm looking for him.

It's Wednesday morning and I'm not due at work until noon. So I'm over on the shoreside part of town, a good way in from the ocean and the beach, in this sort of run-down neighborhood, looking for Stuey.

For some reason all the houses over here look the same—like cracker boxes set on end, three stories high and six to the block, built of wood and painted in faded grays and muddy browns that peel off their sides in long strips.

But for all their sameness, it isn't hard figuring out which house is Stuey's.

As you approach his block, you can hear the music—Jimi Hendrix or Jimmy Page or some other mad guitar man—just pouring out of this one house, so loud that, like it or not, everybody in the neighborhood must be vibrating to it.

I follow the sound to the basement of a house two down from the end of the block.

I wait until whichever mad guitar player it is pauses for breath and then I bang hard on the door and—as fast as that—the music cuts off.

I get a sudden flash that I've got the wrong door of the wrong house and that the wrong guy is about to swing this door open and he's going to be really pissed and—

"Holly!"

"Oh! Stuey! Hi!"

He's standing there in a pair of cutoff jeans, barefoot, stripped to the waist and drenched with sweat and looking at me like I just dropped in from another planet.

"Hi," he says. "What—uh?"

And like I just dropped in from another planet, I tell him, "My father kicked us out of where we were rehearsing, which was upstairs in my brother Bryan's room, because of how the neighbors next door, who vote in elections, were calling up the dispatcher and complaining

128

about the noise and everything, which isn't your problem, of course—or shouldn't be, anyway, unless . . .''

My spaceship runs out of gas.

Stuey offers me a lift.

"You want to come in?" he says.

"Yes," I say, "if it's okay."

"You'll feel right at home," he says.

He smiles and swings his door open.

I tell him, "Thanks," and step inside.

I guess it's Bryan's room that Stuey's thinking of, the way it looked when he brought up Eddie's drums, because his place—I think his father lives here, too, but I don't see any sign of him—it's like a cave and an attic and a ship's galley and a used clothing store all rolled into one.

And a recording studio. The music that was flooding the street outside must have come out of these two giant speakers that he's got hung from the ceiling.

I look around to see—

"What are you looking for?" he asks me.

"The music," I tell him. "Was it Hendrix? Or Jimmy Page? Clapton?"

He laughs. "Hendrix," he says.

"Tape or—?"

"CD," he says.

"I thought so," I tell him. "What album?"

"I forget," he says. "They're all in each other's boxes, so . . .''

"It sounded great," I tell him.

"Yeah," he says.

"Yeah."

"So—uh?" he says.

"Why I'm here?" I ask him.

"Yeah," he says. "Unless it's a secret."

I laugh. "No, it's—"

I don't know how to say it.

So I just say, "Thank you."

And he looks at me.

129

"For helping us out," I explain, "me and—"

"No big deal," he says.

"It *is,* though," I tell him.

"No," he says.

"I don't know what we did to deserve it," I admit, "but—"

"Nothing," he says.

"Yeah," I tell him. "That's what *I* thought."

He smiles.

"And I'm not expecting nothing, either," he says, "if that's what you're worried about."

"No," I lie. "I'm not worried. Do I look worried?"

I give him my "What, me worry?" look.

He recognizes it and laughs.

"No," he says. "You don't."

"I'm not," I say. "It's just . . ."

"The way I feel about it," he says, "the music, rock 'n' roll, it belongs to whoever needs it the most—black folks, white trash, kids, or girls, it doesn't matter."

I look at him.

"That day at Avery's," he says, "when you were asking—you and Claudia—about girls being in the Play-offs, how there hasn't been that many of them and everything . . . ?"

"Yeah . . . ?"

"I thought, Come to think of it! Yeah! John Lennon had it right, all along. Women *are* the niggers of the world.

"But with music," he says, "it's like with everything else—the wise guys who run the show, instead of just ripping it off, they get to thinking that they own it, you know? And it pisses me off. Excuse me."

"Don't be a jerk," I tell him.

He's actually embarrassed!

"Well . . . ," he says.

"The music," I remind him.

"Yeah," he says. "But if I get a chance to remind

130

them—the wise guys—who the music used to belong to and who it belongs to still . . ."

He shrugs and grins.

"It's like I'm returning it to its rightful owners," he says. "It's like—I don't know. It makes me feel like Robin Hood, you know?"

He laughs and shakes his head.

"And a guy like me," he says, "I don't get that many chances to feel like that, so . . ."

He's been looking at the floor through most of this. But now, smiling like he's embarrassed at saying as much as he has, he looks up at me, and he says, "So what can I do for you, Holly?"

> *"I wanna be a rock—*
> *Wanna be a rock—*
> *Wanna be a rock, rock, rock 'n' roll star.*
> *Watch out!"*

Four-thirty, Wednesday afternoon.

Claudia and Mary Ellen and I are up on the stage at the Cobblestone Inn, singing and playing and dancing our little hearts out. We've been at it for almost an hour now. It's been really great. And we owe it all to Stuey.

It was his idea, rehearsing at the Cobblestone. Since it was just standing here empty all day anyway, he said, and since his boss, Arthur Kilburn, never comes in until after dinner, and since he, Stuey, comes in early every day to check out the sound and the lights and everything and get set up for the night, it wouldn't be any problem for him to just open the door for us and let us in.

I could have kissed him, almost. But I just said, "Thanks, Stuey," and I meant it and that seemed to be good enough.

Alice, thank goodness, when I asked her if I could work breakfasts for the next three weeks, up until Labor Day

Weekend, and take off earlier in the afternoon, so I could get to rehearsals by three-thirty, Alice understood.

Claudia's boss at the Audio Vault let her shift her schedule around, too, so she'll be working more nights, which means that she'll be seeing less of Eddie, which—if you believe it—is okay with her.

And Mary Ellen, since she isn't working, except for doing volunteer work at her church where she's free to come and go as she pleases, was pleased to come to the Cobblestone Inn this afternoon at three-thirty for the first rehearsal of our new band.

So here we are. And so far, like I said, it's been terrific. We've been terrific. We've been having a lot of fun with each other and making some pretty good music together.

Or at least we thought we were, up until a minute ago when Stuey—who's in the lighting booth, running our lights and mixing our sound—rigged up these monitors so that we could hear ourselves, hear what we sound like together, the way that an audience would hear us if they were sitting out front right now.

But since Stuey rigged up the monitors, now that I can actually hear what we sound like together—Boy! Do we sound lousy!

It's like our instruments are tuned to different scales and our voices don't blend with each other, and the song, *Rock 'n' Roll Star,* which we're singing only because I haven't come up with anything better and at least it's original—it really sucks!

And this isn't just what I'm thinking, either. Just looking at Claudia and Mary Ellen, I can see they're feeling the same way that I do, namely, *Ughh!*

So none of us can wait until we get to the end of this thing, and when we get there, as we hit the last note, the relief we feel at having this torture over with is so strong, we all just burst out laughing because—what else can you do?

Except stop dead, which is what we do when we hear someone at the back of the room, clapping his hands and laughing along.

132

"You've got guts," he says. "I'll give you that!"

And now, as he steps out of the shadows and moves toward the stage, I see that he's Arthur Kilburn, and I think, *"Oh-oh, We're in trouble!"*

"But what is this?" he says. "How'd you get in?"

"It was me," says Stuey, stepping out from the lighting booth. "I told them, as long as I was here getting the place ready to open, if they didn't get in the way, it'd be okay."

Arthur just looks at him.

"We needed a place to rehearse," I tell him.

He looks at me, like I must be joking.

"For what?" he says. "Are the Brownies having a dance?"

He laughs at that.

"No," I tell him. "For the Playoffs."

He *really* laughs at that.

"Just to be in them," Claudia explains.

"No way!" I tell her. "We're in it to win!"

"Whatever," she says.

I swear, I could—!

"Well," says Arthur, "I suppose the crowd could use a good laugh. I'm just afraid, if somebody's got a weak stomach, you know, it could get ugly."

"We've only just started," I tell him. "We'll get better."

"By next Monday night?" he asks me. "Or the Monday night after that? That's all the time you got, you know. The week before the Showdown, we're dark that Monday night."

"I know," I tell him, although I'd actually forgotten that the Playoffs skipped the last Monday before the Showdown. "We'll be ready," I tell him.

He shakes his head.

"If you say so," he says. "But if I was you, I'd stick to the Brownie dances. You'll get a lot more respect there. You know what I mean? Instead of people laughing you off the stage.

"Think about it," he says. "And then, if you still feel

133

like you want to cut your throats in public, let me know, and I'll get your pal Stuey here to sharpen up the razor for you. Okay?''

He turns to go.

"Oh!" he says.

He turns back to me.

"And do me a favor?" he says. "Wait'll I get downstairs and into my office with the door closed before you start playing again?"

I just look at him.

"Thanks," he says.

And off he goes like a sadistic Santa, laughing all the way.

And as soon as he's out of earshot, because I'm so pissed I can't wait until he's gone, I wheel on Claudia and, screaming at her as quietly as I can, I ask her, "What was that?!!''

"What?" she says, looking surprised and like she can't imagine what I'm talking about.

"What?" I ask her.

"Yeah," she says, as dumb as before. "What?"

"What was all that about us just being in it to be in it?" I ask her.

She gets it.

"Oh," she says and, cocking her head to one side, she looks me in the eyes and she says, "You heard us, didn't you?"

Like she's conducting a poll.

"Yes," I admit, "but—"

"And you heard Bent?" she asks me.

"Yes . . ."

"And you heard the bands last week?"

"Two of them."

"Any good?"

I answer with a sigh.

"That's what all that was about," she says.

"We're still just learning the song," says Mary Ellen.

134

Like we'd both forgotten that Mary Ellen was there, Claudia and I turn and look at her.

"Are we *that* bad?" she asks.

I look at Claudia.

She's looking at me, waiting to see if I'm ready to face the awful truth.

"Well . . . ," I say, working my way up to it.

"Want to try something?" says Stuey.

I'd forgotten him, too.

"Like what?" I ask him. He was standing down at the foot of the stage. "Arsenic?"

He laughs.

"Nice that somebody can!" I think.

"No," he says. "Just run through the song again, okay?"

I look at him.

"You mean like getting back on the horse?" says Mary Ellen.

He looks at her.

"Sort of," he says.

"It's okay with me," I tell him.

I look at Claudia.

She shrugs. "If you can take it," she says, "I guess I can."

"Okay," says Stuey. "Just give me a second."

And that's about what it takes—a second's worth of Stuey darting around, running back into the lighting booth, popping backstage, chasing all over the place, doing I don't know what, but lots of it and very fast.

And then, before we know it, here's his voice, crackling over the speakers, saying, "Okay, guys! Whenever you're ready . . ."

I don't know where he's talking from, but after exchanging a glance and a shrug with my partners, I lean into the mike and I say, "Okay."

Then, turning to Claudia and Mary Ellen, like I've just come up with a really original idea, I say, "What do you say we try it, just this once, with everybody listening to what everybody else is playing and trying to fit what they're playing in with it? Okay?"

Claudia and Mary Ellen exchange a glance and a grin, and then, Mary Ellen nods and says, "Okay, boss."

And "Okay, boss," says Claudia.

I feel my face go red.

"Okay," I say.

I look at my shoes.

"Would you count off, please, boss?" says Claudia.

"Please?" says Mary Ellen.

I shake my head and, like I'm talking to myself, I say, "Bitches!"

They laugh.

I look up and, setting up the tempo, I count off, "Uh-one, two, hey-what's-new and . . ."

Bloo-wheee!

It hits an instant before the beat, a split second before the rest of us, this guitar chord from out of nowhere— *Jasper?!*—this phenomenal gusher of sound that hits at the base of your spine and shoots up your back and explodes out the top of your head!

And here we come, a split second later

"*I wanna be a rock 'n' roll star . . .*"

Jumping in, playing and singing, racing to catch up.

And this guitar from nowhere—*Hendrix?!*—it keeps on coming. It doesn't quit.

Bloo-wheee!

And suddenly, none of us can believe what we're hearing through our monitors!

Don't look now, folks, but with this phantom guitar charging straight up the middle and the rest of us falling into place around it, we sound like a band!

Bloo-wheee!

"*Jimmy Page?*" I wonder. "*Eric Clapt—?*"

Suddenly, it hits me.

I look toward the lighting booth.

No sign of Stuey in there.

No sign of him out front, either.

Backstage?

I look into the wings.

Nothing.

I pick up my microphone, lift it out of its stand and, still singing, I mosey over to the side of the stage, peek around the curtain, and look backstage.

And there he is!

Too into it to notice me and too into it to quit, Stuey is bent over backwards with his eyes on the ceiling and his head in the clouds, wailing away on a red Stratocaster, making the kind of music, *the exact kind of music* that blew me away when I went looking for him the other day, *the exact kind of music* that was pouring out over the street, playing out of those two huge speakers—*Hendrix* music, *Clapton* music and, no doubt about it now, *Stuey* music!

I stop singing.

Stuey stops playing.

Out from behind her drums, suddenly, standing behind me and leaning over my shoulder, Claudia says, "Wow!"

Looming over both of us, her stick propped like a rifle over her shoulder, Mary Ellen says, "Me, too!"

"That was you the other day," I say. "Not Hendrix."

Stuey turns to face me. He's grinning from ear to ear.

"Hendrix is dead," he says.

"No way!" says Jasper.

He's standing behind Mary Ellen, looking over her shoulder, smiling at me.

"So what do we do now, boss?" asks Mary Ellen.

I look at her.

"He's one of *them*," Claudia reminds me.

"One of who?" asks Stuey.

"Boys," I tell him.

"Oh! Yeah," he says. "I am."

"Are we against boys?" asks Mary Ellen.

Claudia heaves a sigh. "Not lately," she says.

Mary Ellen cracks up.

Jasper growls like Roy Orbison on "Pretty Woman."

I shoot him a look.

"I thought—" I say. *"We* thought—Claudia and me— we thought it would be better if we could do it on our own."

"Takes a big gal to admit she's wrong," says Jasper.

I curl my lip at him.

"Some kind of political thing?" asks Mary Ellen.

"Some kind of something," I tell her.

And then, turning back to Stuey and looking him in the eye, I say, "You sure?"

He glances down at his crotch, looks up at me, and says, "Last time I looked."

I break up.

Everybody does.

I tell Stuey, "You'll do," and I hold out my hand to him.

He grins and takes my hand and gives it a shake.

"Rock 'n' roll," he says.

"Rock 'n' roll," shouts Mary Ellen.

"Rock 'n' roll!" shouts Claudia.

"Rock 'n' roll!" we all shout.

"Rock 'n' roll!!"

TWENTY-NINE

The idea was Jasper's—that we should see what it was like, playing together in front of an audience, at least once before next weekend when we're planning to get up on the stage at the Cobblestone and compete in the Playoffs.

It was Stuey who came up with a place that was willing to let us open tonight, Sunday night, for a garage band called Bunko that's set to open for a neighborhood band called 4X4.

It's called The Fish Pot, this place. It's in Matawan. And when Stuey told us about it, I just naturally supposed that it was a nightclub or a restaurant, at least.

But what it turns out to be is a clam bar—the kind of place where overweight people in too tight clothes go to eat buckets of clams and drink pitchers of beer and shout to each other over the music.

We're the music. Me and my troops—Claudia, Mary Ellen, Stuey, and me. We're all out in this storage shed that's attached to the rear of the place, milling around and tuning up, being nervous and acting cocky, and generally getting set to go on.

"Does anybody smell fish?" asks Mary Ellen.

And since that's practically all that we've been talking about since we got here more than an hour ago, how the place totally reeks of fish, we all break up.

And then we go back to milling around, etc.

I bought a new outfit for tonight. Jasper thought that it might help me get into the right frame of mind, if I put on something I'd never worn before. He thought that it might help me become someone I've never been before.

What I went for was—well, first I saw this ankle-length cotton print skirt, like you'd wear to a square dance. But what it reminded me of was this movie called *The Field*, that was made in Ireland.

It's about the Irish, of course. But it's also got these gypsies in it, including this one gypsy girl, who isn't that pretty—she's got bad teeth and wears nothing but rags down to her ankles—but she's so hot!

So that's what I went for, a modified Irish gypsy look, the ankle-length skirt, a white off-the-shoulder blouse, a red bandanna rolled tight and tied around my neck like a necklace, and, for luck, my mother's hoop earrings, the ones my Aunt Peg gave her, the ones that she only wore when Aunt Peg came to visit.

But then, when Aunt Peg came to visit, and Mom put on the earrings for her, the whole time that she wore them she'd have this little smile on her face, like she was getting away with something, and it made her look so young, Mom, so girlish and beautiful . . .

So that's what I'm wearing when we walk out on stage and introduce ourselves to the audience.

"Hi, everybody," I say, "we're Holly and the Heartbreakers."

I wait a second for the crowd to applaud.

Dream on!

"We'd like to play a couple of songs for you," I continue, nonetheless.

And then, telling myself, *"I'm hot, hot, hot!"* I turn to Claudia and nod. She nods back to me.

And we begin—

> *B'dee-bah-bah-bah*
> *Thump!*
> *B'dee-bah-bah . . .*

When we finish, a lifetime later, and nobody in the crowd seems to notice or care, I look around to see what's become of Stuey and Mary Ellen, who started the number standing just a little behind me.

I find them cowering at the back of the stage, huddled around Claudia, practically sitting on her drums.

Joining them, I say, "Okay, so they're not Stones' fans!"

"But then again . . ." says Stuey.

"Well," I say, ignoring him, *"Rock n' Roll Star* isn't a Stones song."

"Good point," says Mary Ellen.

"Pisses me off," says Claudia.

"What does?" I ask her.

She nods at the crowd and says, "Them!" And right then, like a boxer coming off the ropes, fighting for his life, fighting for the crown, she rears back and just tears into her drums—

> *Bam!*
> *Bam-bam!*
> *Bamalambam!*
>
> *Bam!*
> *Bam-bam!*
> *Bamalambam!*

And I signal to Stuey—

> *Bloo-wheee*

And here we go again!

> *"I wanna' be a rock n' roll star . . ."*

We're off and running!

"So tough, you never seen nobody tougher . . ."

Smack!
Right into a wall!

"I wanna' be a rock.
Rock around the clock.
I wanna' be a rock, rock, rock n' roll star . . ."

Where we crash.
Ka-boom!
And burn.

"Tonight!"

And get a pretty nice round of applause, which really surprises me, until I turn to my pals and gesture for them to take a bow and see that they're already walking off the stage and that the applause that I'm hearing is for the next band, Bunko, which is already walking on.

And then, because I've got a feeling, if the crowd saw the look on my face they'd laugh their asses off, I don't turn back to look at them.

I just duck my head, and like a rat running from the light, I scurry off the stage and escape into the night.

THIRTY

"**E**ddie's waiting," I tell Claudia.

It can't be more than five minutes since we came off the stage and now, while Stuey helps Mary Ellen wrestle our gear into the van that she's borrowed from her mother, we're keeping out of their way, standing together off to one side, out in The Fish Pot's parking lot.

Glancing over her shoulder and across the lot to where Eddie is leaning against his Cherokee, Claudia turns back to me and says, "Yeah."

I didn't see Eddie inside, but I imagine he was there. I imagine Claudia invited him.

"Did he say anything?" I ask her.

She shakes her head.

"What's to say?" she says.

"Do you think I . . . ?"

"Sucked?" she guesses.

I nod.

She nods and says, "Yeah."

I turn to Stuey.

He nods and says, "Afraid so."

"Mary Ellen?"

She sighs and says, "I hate to go along with the crowd, but . . ."

So it's unanimous.

I sucked.

The big one.

THIRTY-ONE

The fog is so thick—like mist suffused with moon-light—I can't see the moon or the stars or even the sky.

I can't tell where the land ends and where the ocean begins.

There is no sound but the sighing of the wind, the churning of the ocean, the cries of sea birds.

I'm crying, too.

My feet pick their way along the water's edge, walking where the sand is smooth and the water never more than ankle deep.

Where are my shoes?!

"You know what's wrong?" he says.

He's beside me and a little behind me, walking on the beach. His jeans are rolled up around his calves. His feet are bare.

I want to sob and cry out, *"Everything!"*

I tell myself I mustn't, but even as I do, I hear myself sobbing and crying out—"Everything!"

It's like a nightmare!

"But mostly?" he says. "What is it mostly?"

"I can't do it!" I cry.

I'm ashamed to admit it and terrified too.

As often as I've said these words to myself, I've hardly ever spoken them out loud. I've always been afraid, if I did, the whole world and everything in it might suddenly disappear, and I'd be left alone with nothing but the sound of my own words, echoing back to me—"I can't! I can't! I can't!"—from the endless emptiness of the universe.

"What?" he says. "What is it that you can't do?"

"Make you want me!" I cry. "You or anybody else! I can't! I've tried. I've tried and tried, but—it's no use! I can't! I can't! I—"

"Whoops!" he says.

I turn to look at him and—*Whoops!*—my feet fly out from under me.

"Aagh!"

God! The water! It's so cold!

"Oww!"

And hard!

A rock! I've landed on a rock and—

"Ooh!"

I've stubbed my toe, skinned it.

I'm bleeding!

"Here," he says.

He reaches his hand out to me.

I've got a feeling that he tripped me, although it's hard to imagine how he could have. But I'm soaked through and I'm freezing and shivering, so . . .

I take his hand.

He smiles and helps me to my feet.

"You're cold," he says.

He's looking at my breasts.

Through my blouse, he can see my nipples.

"Come," he says. "There's a fire."

I look up at him.

He's looking down the beach.

I follow his gaze and there, where I saw nothing before but fog and more fog, I see a bonfire blazing and the night breeze stirring its flames, throwing handfuls of sparks high in the air.

I want to ask Jasper about it—where it came from, why I didn't see it before. But as I turn to ask him, I feel his arm slipping around my shoulder. I feel myself being enfolded in his cape. And instantly . . .

I'm warm.

My clothes are dry.

Someone is singing.

> *"Slow and easy, baby . . ."*

If I didn't know better, I'd swear it was me.

> *"Slow and easy . . ."*

And we're dancing, Jasper and I—

> *"Take your time, girl."*

Dancing around the fire—

> *"Wait and see . . ."*

Arms outstretched, holding hands, looking into each other's eyes—

> *"I was doing fine*
> *Until your eyes met mine,*
> *Now, suddenly—*
> *Ecstasy . . ."*

Turning, first slowly—

> *"Ecstasy, my darling,*
> *Ecstasy.*
> *It's like a fire raging*
> *Deep inside of me . . ."*

Now, faster—

> *"And I could fight the fire,*
> *But why deny desire,*
> *When it's meant to be?*
> *Ecstasy . . ."*

Spinning, the two of us, now apart, now together—
"Jasper . . ."
"Shhh . . ."
Spinning, two as one, now together, now apart—
"Please . . ."
"Shhh . . ."
Spinning, 'round and 'round, faster and faster—
"I'm afraid . . ."
"Don't be . . ."
Leaning back in his arms—
"I've got you . . ."
So far back—
"I can't . . ."
I fear I'll fall—
"You can . . ."
But, no—
"Yes!"
I'm flying!
"Yes!"
Up in the air.
Over the fire.
Higher and higher.
Higher and higher.
Up and up and up, so high.
I toss back my head—

> *"Ecstasy!"*

And laugh aloud—

> *"Ecstasy!"*

At the vast and fathomless—

> *"Ecstasy!"*

Sky!

THIRTY-TWO

"It's prohibited."

"Pop!"

He's standing over me, looking down at me.

"It's prohibited by law," he says, "sleeping on the beach."

I start to explain.

"I didn't mean to—"

"Especially," he says, "when you've got a nice warm—well, you *had* a nice bed waiting for you at home! Get up, would you?"

"Yeah," I tell him.

I get to my feet and brush the sand from my skirt. But the smile on my face and the memory of what put it there—*Wow! What a dream*—that, I can't brush off so easily.

Where are my shoes?!

Ah! There, behind my driftwood pillow.

My toe!

Where I stubbed it, it isn't skinned or even sore.

"Come on," says Pop.

He sets out, walking up the beach toward the street where he's left his cruiser parked and waiting.

"How did you know . . . ?" I ask him.

"Claudia," he says.

"Oh . . ."

"She said you'd had a rough night, last night," he says, "over in Matawan."

"Yeah."

"Me, too," he says.

I look over at him.

His eyes are on his shoes.

"I'm sorry," I tell him.

"In fact," he says, "I can't say that I've had that many good nights since I got that disturbing-the-peace call, back a week or so ago.

"I'm not in the habit of striking women," he says. "Least of all my own daughter.

"It's something that I've been proud of," he says. "The times that I laid into your brothers, I never once raised a hand to you."

"Or reached out a hand, either," I remind him.

He sighs a heavy sigh.

And then, nodding, he says, "I've never been good with women. All my life. Only just your mother, God rest her soul.

"And your aunt Peg," he says. "We get along. But otherwise . . ." He shakes his head.

"I don't know what the trouble is," he says. "If it's the fear of God that the nuns put into me or what. But I've never been myself when there were women around so . . ."

"So you take a powder," I say.

I try to make it like a joke, but it comes out more bitter than I intended.

"I suppose, yes," says Pop. "You could say that."

"I could, yeah," I say. "I mean, you've only been doing it forever."

"Not forever," he says. "Just since your mother . . ."

He doesn't understand!

"That's forever, Pop!" I tell him. "That's forever!"

He's surprised at how upset I am.

"Sure it is," he says, trying to calm me but thinking about it, too. "Sure it is."

"Not that it makes a lot of difference now," I tell him. "But I used to think that I had something terrible."

"What do you mean?" he says.

"Some disease or curse or something—"

"Who told you that?" he says.

"Nobody!" I tell him. "But I knew."

"There was never any such thing!" he says.

"I used to beg Bryan to tell me what it was, but he wouldn't tell me. He'd just tease me."

"There was nothing wrong with you then," says Pop, "and there's nothing wrong with you now."

"I'm glad to hear it," I tell him.

"I'm proud of you," he insists.

"Pop!" I say, like *"Please!"*

"But I am," he says. "Jesus! Most of these kids that I see out here—summer kids, too, with all the advantages— they're just running wild, most of them, day and night. They've got that little respect for themselves or anybody else.

"But you—with your mother taken early and but little help from me, like you say—you're solid. And don't tell me no, because I see you going right at it, sticking right to it. Even this rock and roll business—though I don't pretend to like it, and I can't see where it will get you, besides Matawan."

I laugh.

"I don't either, Pop. Maybe nowhere, maybe some- where. I don't know. But that's why I don't want to get myself tied down to anything just yet."

"Meaning college, I suppose."

I nod and tell him, "Meaning college."

"I don't think of college as tying you down," he says. "I think of it as turning you loose to do whatever you choose to.

"That's how your mother saw it, too," he says. "Those

are her earrings you're wearing, aren't they? The ones that Peggy gave her. Pretty on you . . .''

"Thanks, Pop."

"But if you could see it that way, too . . ." he says.

"I'll try, Pop."

"That's all I'm asking," he says. "Lift?"

We've arrived at his cruiser.

I shake my head and tell him, "No thanks, Pop. I need to walk."

"Sure," he says. "Good for you."

"Yeah," I tell him.

"Well . . ." he says.

And I say "Thanks," and I kiss his cheek and, quick, before the shock wears off, I turn around and walk away.

THIRTY-THREE

"Where you going?" Claudia wants to know.

It's Monday night, Playoff night.

"I need some air," I tell her.

We're standing in the kitchen at the Cobblestone, waiting to go on.

"We're next," Mary Ellen reminds me.

Out in the show room, Chain Saw Massacre, the fifth band on the bill, is tearing through something or other—I hate to think what.

"I know," I tell her, "but those French fries . . ."

How long it's been since they changed the oil in the deep fryer is another thing that I hate to think about.

"You want me to come with you?" asks Claudia.

The way she's looking at me, I can see that she's worried about me.

"No," I tell her. "I'm okay."

She doesn't believe me—any more than I do—but she nods and says, "Okay."

"Hey, Holly?"

As I head for the door, Stuey calls to me. I stop and look back at him.

"You look great," he says.

Standing there, looking back over my shoulder at him, with my hair pulled back tight in a French knot and my mother's hoop earrings dangling from my ears, wearing this little halter top and these lace-edged Spandex bicycle shorts, I probably look like a girl with nothing on her mind but sex.

But right this second, what's on my mind is the spaghetti that's sitting like a lump in my stomach.

So I tell Stuey, "Thanks," and, as fast as I can, I beat it out the door.

Wow!

As I hit the alley, I close my eyes and lean back against the wall.

I should have skipped dinner. I knew it!

But when Claudia's friend Laird showed up at the house this afternoon—after our final rehearsal, which we held up in Bryan's room, after I asked Pop and he said it would be okay—carrying a big bowl of whole wheat spaghetti *primavera* that she'd made, I didn't have the heart.

"Complex carbohydrates," she said. "The best thing for you."

Only now, with the fan over the kitchen door blowing the stench from the kitchen into the alley where it mixes and mingles with the stench rising from the garbage cans that line the walls, I'm thinking how nice it would be if I could just climb into one of these cans, curl up inside it, pull the lid over my head, and die.

Why is this happening?! After this afternoon's re-

hearsal, the way that I was singing, like never before, so strong and sure? When I finished, Stuey just looked at me like he was amazed and said, "Where you been hiding her?" And Mary Ellen said, "Smokin'!" And Claudia just said, "Holls!" like she couldn't believe it.

So why, if I was so hot and cocky this afternoon, why is it that now I'm feeling so incredibly sick and so . . .

"Scared?"

A voice jumps out of the shadows.

"Who's that?!"

"Me," says Jasper, stepping out into the light.

"Oh," I say, trying to sound like, *"Sure! Who else?"*

But Jasper, seeing how relieved I am that it's only him, says, "I'm sorry."

"No," I tell him. "It's okay. It's just—. What am I going to do, Jasper!"

"Holly . . ." he says.

He's trying to calm me, but—

"All those people in there!" I cry, thinking about the crowd in the club. "And them in there!" I wail, thinking about the crowd in the kitchen. "And you!" I sob. "What's going to happen to you, if I don't . . . ?"

"Shhh . . . ," he says.

He puts his finger to my lips. And I swear, even though I know that I can't actually *feel* his finger touching my lips, I feel *something*—like a *warmth* that's, like, *comforting*—just as if I *could* feel his finger touching my lips.

"Take it easy," he says.

I shake my head and tell him, "I can't."

"Scared is part of the trip," he says.

I look at him.

"It is!" he says. "All the times I went out there?"

"Yeah . . ."

"There wasn't one time that I wasn't as scared as you are right now."

"Jasper!"

"No! It's true," he says. "And not just me. Most ev-

153

erybody. Scared is okay. It's what gets your adrenaline pumping."

"It's what makes me wet my pants!" I tell him.

He laughs.

"The mistake that people make," he says, "is thinking because they're scared, it means that they're no good, when it's really nothing but their adrenal glands pumping, getting them fueled up for the big lift-off."

"How bad are we?" I ask him.

He laughs.

"Honestly?" I insist.

"Honestly," he says. "You've come a really long way in a really short time and, as of this afternoon's rehearsal, I'd say that you and your friends are as good as a lot of the better bar bands I've seen—including some that I was in."

"And the new song?" I ask him.

"Good," he says.

"Not terrific?"

"Good enough," he says.

"And the way I look?"

"Terrific," he says.

"Hot?"

"Smokin'," he says.

"You wouldn't kid me?"

He grins. "I give you my word," he says.

"I guess that ought to be good enough," I sigh.

He shakes his head.

"Don't worry," he says. "In a couple of minutes, all of this will be behind you. I promise you. The minute you walk out onto that stage and see the audience sitting out there, you're going to get such a rush, you'll kick right into overdrive. And the next thing you know—you and your troops—you'll be spittin' fire and kickin' ass and feeling good like you wouldn't believe!"

I look him in the eye and tell him, "I want to believe you."

"Why don't you, then?" he says, looking right back at me, looking deep into my eyes.

"After all," he says, "isn't that the way it goes? One minute, you feel like you might drown. And the next minute, you're dancing on air. And the minute after that, it's—"

It's almost like we say it together, only with me saying it first, a split second before he does—

"Ecstasy!"

"Yes," he says, smiling a slow smile at me and nodding his head.

And even though I'm not sure exactly what it means—what is real and what are dreams—for just this second, standing there, with his eyes on mine and my heart in my throat, pounding like a drum, I couldn't care less.

"Holly?"

Claudia is standing in the doorway.

"Ready?" I ask her.

"Yes," she says.

I nod to her and tell her, "Let's do it!"

THIRTY-FOUR

"Ever seen legs like these?"

I hit the high one and hold it.

"Legs like these?"

Mary Ellen chimes in with her bluesy note.

"Legs like these?"

Claudia adds the eerie one that curls your toes and kicks in with the bass drum.

Thump-thump-thump-thump . . .

Riding in on his trusty guitar, Stuey takes a run up a rainbow and leaps into space in an arching, aching, swirling dazzle of polyphonic flight.

Bo-wah
B'lee-ah-b'lee-ah-b'lee-ah
F'wee-ee-ee-ee-ee-ee-eeeee . . .

Now, everybody comes together, chugging with the rhythm, laying down a bed to boogie on.

Ch'dong-dong-digga-dong
Dong-dong-digga-dong
Dong-dong

Modulating our voices, we swoop up a tone and a half to a killer chord—

"Eat—
Eat—
Eat—"

Shatter it—

"—your heart out!"

And cut if off, clean.

Now, we stand, stone still, in total silence, poised on the brink.

And the Monday night crowd gathered at the Cobblestone Inn for the season's final Famous Amateur Night Playoffs just bursts into applause!

And the rush!

The kick!

The absolute thrill of it!

It's just like Jasper said!

Claudia, Mary Ellen, Stuey, and I, we all look at one another and extend the moment for a moment longer and a moment beyond that and then, on my signal, we stuff it!

> *Ch'dong-dong-digga-dong*
> *Dong-dong-digga-dong*
> *Dong-dong.*

> *Ch'dong-dong-digga-dong*
> *Dong-dong-digga-dong*
> *Dong-dong . . .*

Now, as Stuey and Mary Ellen take a step back, I take a step forward and, telling myself that I'm hot—as hot as a gypsy girl dancing barefoot on a beach, as hot as a blazing bonfire stirred by an ocean breeze—I grab the microphone with both hands and I sing—

> *"Ever seen*
> *Legs like these*
> *'Pretty please.'*
> *Mister—"*

And Claudia and Mary Ellen, looking hot and willing in their halter tops and bicycle shorts, come knifing in—

> *"Eat—*
> *Eat—*
> *Eat—*
> *—your heart out!"*

And again, the crowd explodes with applause, only this time it's twice as loud as before.

But this time, since we can't stop and wait for them to quit, I ride right on over them, singing—

> *"Tangerines?*
> *Wanna squeeze?*
> *On your knees,*
> *Mister.*
> *Eat—*
> *Eat—*
> *Eat—*
> *—your heart out!"*

And then, with Claudia and Mary Ellen helping me out on the vocals, Stuey supplying the instrumental fireworks, and all of us pouring our hearts and souls into it, we go on with us and the crowd feeding off each other, pushing each other higher and higher until at the end we're all of us together, up on our feet, dancing and shouting—

> *"Eat—*
> *Eat—*
> *Eat—*
> *Eat—*
> *Eat—*
> *—your heart out!!!"*

Stuey and Claudia wrap it up with a—

> *F'wee-eeeet!*

And a—

> *Thump!*

And—*God!*—it's like a clap of thunder, the roar of the crowd, the way it explodes all around us!

Whistling, shouting, cheering, stomping!

More and more and more!

I'm in heaven!

I mean it! I feel so fabulous—so full and fine—I want to kiss everybody in sight! Claudia! Mary Ellen! Stuey! Jasper!

Especially Jasper, who stands on the dance floor right in front of the stage, grinning from ear to ear, his hands raised over his head, leading the crowd's applause like, in the excitement, he's totally forgotten that nobody but me can see him!

But before I can kiss anybody at all, here comes Arthur Kilburn, charging up onto the stage, looking surprised— or is it upset?

And holding both hands up over his head, palms out, like he's signaling the crowd to hold their applause, he shouts, "Okay! Okay! Let's bring 'em all back out again, okay? Come on, fellas! Come on out!"

And turning to the bands standing offstage in the wings, he motions for them to come out onto the bandstand.

And as they come out, riding on what's left of our applause, Arthur turns back to the audience and says, "In just a second, I'm going to ask you to decide which one of these terrific bands is gonna move on to the Showdown—which, I want to remind you, will be held right here on this stage just one week from this coming Saturday night—but first, I want to tell you about a little surprise we've cooked up that I want you guys to be the first to know about."

As the bandstand fills up with bodies and the applause dies away to nothing, I look over at Claudia, and she looks back at me, and all of us—Stuey and Mary Ellen on the bandstand and Jasper in front of it—we look at each other, thinking, if only Arthur would shut up and let the crowd make its choice, we could have this thing wrapped up. But—

"Before Don Harmon breaks the news on his show tomorrow morning," he says, "and before that phone over there starts ringing off the hook with people begging me for reservations, I want you guys to know that this year's panel of judges—which includes Peter Karl of ENO Records and Walter Scott of WJRZ-FM and yours truly, of course—will be headed by none other than the biggest rock 'n' roll star to come out of anywhere, since The King himself came storming out of Memphis, Tennessee.

"Yes!" he says. "That's right!" he shouts. "The man that I'm talking about is nobody else but Wildwood's very own—Joey Doyle!!"

And I can't tell you! The way that the girls scream and the guys go wild, it's actually scary!

And me, I admit it, as pissed as I was just a second ago that Arthur was taking forever to get down to business, right this second, thinking about Joey Doyle coming back to Wildwood for the first time in five or six years, and us performing for him on the very same stage where he was discovered, and him discovering us, and us getting to meet him and everything, it's just too much!

I mean, I'm that close to screaming and jumping up and down myself, but—

"Okay," says Arthur, shushing the crowd. "Okay! So now you know. So let's get back to the business at hand—picking the winner of tonight's running of the Cobblestone's World Famous Amateur Night Playoffs!"

As the crowd breaks into applause, Arthur squeezes through the mob onstage and works his way over to the far side of the bandstand where, holding his hand over the head of this pasty-faced guy with this slash of purple lipstick where his mouth should be, he turns to the audience and shouts the name of the guy's band.

"Scarlatti!" he shouts.

And the crowd applauds.

And Arthur moves on to the next guy, an electric cowboy, a dude in Justin boots and a Stetson hat.

Stretching up on tiptoes, Arthur holds his hand over his head and shouts the name of his band. "Red-Eye!"

And the crowd applauds a little louder.

And Arthur moves on, working his way across the stage, saving us for last. "Rambo!" he shouts.

And the crowd applauds again—not quite so loud or long this time.

But now, as he shouts, "Chain-Saw Massacre!" the crowd lets loose with a real ovation.

And while the ovation is still building and even before it peaks, Arthur moves over to me.

And as quick as a magician picking a card out of the air, he passes his hand over my head and says, "Holly and the Heartbreakers," in a whisper so low that I swear nobody in the world, not even a bat, could hear it!

Except—

"Holl—*eee!!!*" A voice rings out from the back of the room.

Laird!

I see her, standing on her chair, fist in the air, shouting our name.

And suddenly—

"Holl-*eee!!* Holl-*eee!!!* Holl-*eee!!*"

A bunch of other voices pick it up.

And the next thing I know, everybody's climbing up on their chairs, raising their fists in the air, shouting my name, applauding and cheering.

And I look over at Arthur, standing beside me.

And he gives me this crooked little grin and this kind of shrug, like *"Oh, well."*

And taking my wrist in his hand, he says, "And the winner is . . ."

And raising my hand in the air, he shouts, "Holly and the Heartbreakers!"

161

THIRTY-FIVE

We've won!!!

We've won!!!

The jukebox kicks in with, *We Are the Champions* and all of us, everybody, the crowd and my crew—Claudia and Stuey and Mary Ellen—we all go bananas!

Jasper!

I look for him at the front of the stage, but he isn't—

Whoa!

Somebody grabs me—"Mary Ellen!"—and lifts me up in the air and swings me around.

And while Mary Ellen's swinging me like I'm on a parachute ride in an amusement park, out of the corner of my eye I see Claudia looking out into the crowd with this worried look on her face.

"Whoa!" I call to Mary Ellen, and as she sets me down and gives me a hug, I tell her, "Way to go!"

"Not so bad yourself," she says.

I turn to Claudia.

"Hey!" I say, "What's—?"

I look where she's looking, across the room to where Terry Kincaid is making his way through the crowd with Eddie Ballard tagging along beside him—and my missing person, Jasper Rollins, tagging after them—making his way toward Arthur Kilburn, who's standing at the bar.

"I guess they're going to drop out," I tell Claudia, "now that they see what they're up against."

It's supposed to be a joke, of course.

But Claudia doesn't laugh.

Eddie does, though. When I turn back to look toward the bar, he's cackling away at some crack that Terry must have made to Arthur, something he said about us, I'd guess, something rotten.

But—*Jesus!*—look at Arthur, now, pointing his finger in Terry's face and giving out to him like you'd think he'd insulted his mother or something!

"What do you suppose is eating him?" I ask Claudia.

"Beats me," she says.

"Are we great or what?" says Stuey.

"Hey!" I say.

Making myself a note to ask Jasper what it was that Terry said that got Arthur so steamed, I turn to greet Stuey.

As he wraps his arms around me and squeezes me tight, I tell him, "We're great!"

"Ay-John!" he says.

"Or what," says Claudia, taking the second choice and fending Stuey off as he releases me and reaches for her.

"Yo!" says Mary Ellen. "Stuey, babes!"

As Mary Ellen offers herself up to Stuey's embrace, I hear Eddie saying, "We gotta' talk."

I turn and see him, standing at the foot of the bandstand, looking up at Claudia.

You'd think that he'd be telling her, "Congratulations," or "Good going!" or something.

You'd think that he'd be proud of her or happy for her.

But all he says is, "Come on."

And from the expression on his face as he nods toward the door, you can see that he's pissed at her—like she's done something wrong!

And Claudia, when Eddie turns his back on her and heads for the door—

"Hey!" I call to her as she starts to go after him. "Where you going?"

She stops and turns back to me.

163

"You're not leaving?" I insist. "We've got some serious partying to do here!"

"I've got to see what's wrong with Eddie," she says.

I can't believe her!

"What's *right* with Eddie?" I ask her.

"Maybe we'll come back," she says.

"If he wants to, you mean?"

"You were great," she says.

"You, too," I tell her.

I give her a hug.

"Rock on," she says.

I let her go.

She turns and walks away.

Shit!

"Tsk! Tsk! Tsk!"

Jasper's back.

"Why do guys have to be such dicks?" I ask him.

"Say what?" says Stuey.

"Stuey!" I say.

"Say who?" says Mary Ellen.

"Mary Ellen!"

"Anybody want to dance?" asks Stuey, looking at me.

"I—uh—promised a friend," I answer smoothly.

"And you call *us* dicks!" says Jasper, who's back where I left him, standing at the foot of the bandstand, shaking his head at me.

"If you think you're up to it," says Mary Ellen.

Stuey looks at her, like a worm eyeing a bird.

" 'It ain't the meat, it's the motion,' " he tells her.

Jasper breaks up.

"Oo!" says Mary Ellen. "Tell me more!"

As she takes Stuey's hand and leads him toward the dance floor, I break up.

And then, turning back to Jasper, I ask him, "What were Arthur and Terry—?"

He shakes his head.

164

"Not now," he says. "Too many people. Too little time. I'm heading home."

"No!"

"Yes," he insists. "I'll wait up for you."

"But I—"

"This is your party," he says. "Your night to howl. Enjoy it while you've got it. You never know when there will be another one."

But I *do* know when there will be another one!

"Labor Day weekend!" I tell him.

"September four through seven," says a voice behind me.

I turn around and there's Marshall Sayers, a senior at Wildwood High, who's as handsome as a movie star and, up until right now, as far as I'm concerned, as distant as the moon.

"Thank you," I tell him.

"I'm good with dates," he says.

"I'd imagine," I say.

He laughs.

"Would you like to—?"

He nods toward the dance floor.

"Later," says Jasper.

"No!" I say.

I turn to see him already fading, as he waves good-bye.

"No?" says Marshall.

"Doubt about it!" I blurt, as I turn back to Marshall. "No doubt about it, I'd love to—"

I nod toward the dance floor.

He grins and shakes his head and offers me his hand, thank God.

I take it.

He leads me to the dance floor.

And so it begins—my night to howl, courtesy of the late great Jasper Rollins. Starting right then and continuing straight on past closing time, I throw myself into letting myself go, totally, the way that Jasper's taught me to.

I dance every dance with everybody who asks me and, for once in my life, everybody asks me.

I dance with Marshall Sayers. I dance with Stuey a couple of times. I dance with Laird. I dance with—I don't know—everybody!

With Peter Wells, the bull-necked star of the wrestling team.

With Mort Hudson, the computer genius with the purple hair and the scholarship to MIT.

With rich kids, poor kids, white kids, a black kid—Harry Robinson, who keeps the stats for the basketball team and dreams of becoming a sportscaster.

With guys I know from school and guys who went to school with my brothers.

I dance with married guys, divorced guys, guys going through trial separations, guys who came with dates, guys who came alone, guys who came with other guys, guys I've known all my life, and guys I've never met before.

And here's the thing—*all of them, every one of them wants me!*

I swear!

I mean, some of them come right out and say it!

Others just offer me things—compliments, drinks, drugs, rides home, rides to New York City!

It's incredible.

I mean, it's like they all bought the song—and the girl in the song—lock, stock, and barrel.

I mean, they really believe that I'm exactly as desirable and unattainable as she is—that I'm actually her—and it drives them nuts! Mad with desire! And I love it!

I love it!

I mean, I could pretend that I don't, but—no, on second thought, I couldn't! I've waited too long for this and wanted it too much and worked too hard to get it.

So, no, I couldn't pretend that I don't love it.

I love it.

It's fabulous!

It should happen to everybody.

But not now.

This is my turn.

"Holly Hanna, isn't it?"

I don't know what time it is when I hear this voice behind me. Late. Past closing.

I turn and say, "Jim Sweeney?"

He smiles and says, "Yes."

I smile and say, "Dance?"

He grins and says, "Ride?"

He wants to take me for a ride.

Think again, sucker!

I grin and say, "Thank you."

THIRTY-SIX

"Funny," says Jim Sweeney.

He reaches for the key and turns off the ignition.

"I don't know what I could have been thinking about," he says.

We're parked in the driveway at the back of my house.

"When I look at you now—"

Looking over at me, he smiles and shakes his head like he can't get over it, the way that I've grown up since he last saw me the night of Bryan's and Barbara's wedding.

"Was it really just a few weeks ago?" he says.

"Yes," I tell him.

"Amazing!" he says. "You look like a whole different girl!"

"I am," I tell him.

"You look really . . ."

"Hot?" I ask him.

He laughs. "Yes," he says. "That's what I was thinking."

I smile and say, "Uh-huh."

"But I guess—" he says, shaking his head, as he thinks back on that night and tries to explain his behavior.

"You seemed so young," he says, *"Looking,* I mean. And you'd had a drink or two, I guess. So had I, of course.

"But us being, you know, like family and everything, I was afraid if I just said, "Sure!" the way that I wanted to, if I just, like, accepted your invitation and came inside the house with you, and we started, you know, fooling around, and one thing led to another, that maybe, after it was over, you'd—I don't know.

"Sometimes girls—young girls especially, without a lot of experience—sometimes they get kind of carried away and start carrying on and crying and everything, saying that you took advantage of them and, well, you know, with all these stories about date rape and everything—"

He shakes his head.

"So," he says, "even though I might have wanted to, which I did, really a lot, but still, what I felt like I had to do was just put my feelings aside and do what I thought was right for you."

"Oh!" I tell him, like I'm such a sucker for the fake sincere way that he's been gazing into my eyes the whole time that he's been feeding me this line of crap that I actually believe it. "That was so nice of you! Even though it really wasn't necessary."

He looks at me.

I smile at him.

"It isn't like I didn't know what I was doing," I tell him.

He likes the sound of that.

"I'm like the girl in the song," I tell him. "You know—'I'm not as green as I am young'?"

"Sure!" he says, like he could kick himself. "I know now!" And he laughs.

168

"And I have to admit," he says, "seeing you now, I can't imagine how I could have been so stupid. But at the time—"

"Of course!" I tell him, like I understand completely and appreciate enormously the sacrifice that he made by denying himself and by "doing what was right" for me.

"And you're right," I tell him. "It *is* funny—because that night, after you said no, you wouldn't come in—"

I shake my head, as if I were reliving the moment.

"I felt so bad about it," I tell him. "So disappointed, you know?"

He knows. I can see by his expression. He's *so* sympathetic!

"So what I did was—"

I slide over closer to him and rest my hand on his shoulder.

"I imagined that you'd said yes," I tell him.

He looks at me.

"I took your hand, you know?"

I take his hand.

"And I led you across the yard and into the house and up the stairs, all the way up to my brother Bryan's room up in the attic, away from everything and everybody.

"And once we got up there, I closed the door, and I locked it. And I turned around, and you were standing there in the middle of the room.

"So I walked over to you, right up to you. I leaned up against you, and I looked up into your eyes, and you looked down into mine, and you bent down to me and, as you kissed me—

"Close your eyes," I tell him.

"Now?" he asks.

I nod and tell him, "Yes."

He smiles.

And as he closes his eyes, I say, "You closed your eyes."

I slide a little closer to him.

169

"And I pressed myself against you," I tell him. "And as I opened my mouth to your tongue, you slipped your hands into my back pockets and pulled me to you.

"I felt you moving against me, and I couldn't wait, and you couldn't either.

"We wanted each other so bad that, right there, standing right there in the middle of my brother's room, we fumbled and tore at each other's clothes and ran our hands and our tongues all over each other's bodies until—'Oh, God! Jim!'—you lifted me up and eased me down onto you and—'Oh!'

"It felt *sooo* good! The way you rocked me! And rolled me! I cried out your name, again and again, over and over, for what seemed like hours and hours, until—

"I woke up the next morning, sprawled across in my brother's bed, exhausted and smiling like—

"Open your eyes," I tell him.

He opens his eyes.

"I woke up the next morning smiling like I am now," I tell him, "because I knew, after everything that we'd done—and we'd done everything that you can imagine—there wasn't anything more that I wanted from you."

He looks at me.

"I'd gotten you out of my system," I tell him.

He doesn't get it.

"I'd flushed you out of my system," I tell him.

He gets it.

I reach for the door handle and, telling him, "Thanks for the ride, you dick!" I slide back across the front seat, climb out of the car, slam the door behind me, strut across the yard, push through the back door, and march into the house.

Slam!

It isn't until then that I crack a smile.

And I wait until I hear Jim Sweeney starting up his car and tearing out of the driveway, before I bust out laughing and call, "Jasper!"

THIRTY-SEVEN

"**W**ho the hell is Jasper?"

Oh, God! What was I thinking?! I've awakened Pop!

He's standing in his bedroom doorway, halfway down the hall, dressed in just his boxer shorts, squinting at me and scratching his head.

I can see that he's more curious than actually pissed, but under the circumstances, curious is bad enough.

How do I get out of this? What do I tell him?

I tell him, "Sorry, Pop," and I keep on moving down the hall, heading for the stairs.

"I heard that you won," he says.

"Yeah."

"Congratulations!"

"Thanks."

"I wish I could have been there," he says. "But I had a head-on over on Twenty-seven. A real mess, it was."

"That's okay, Pop," I say, as I breeze past him and keep on going.

"So, who's Jasper?" he says.

Who's Jasper?

"Just a guy I met, Pop."

"Did you expect to meet him here?" he asks me.

Where's Jasper?

"No, Pop."

As I reach the foot of the stairs, he says, "Hold it!"

Oh, boy!

I stop and turn to him.

"Yes, Pop?"

"This fella' Jasper that you met, what is it that makes you so crazy about him, you need to shout his name out loud when you come waltzing into my house at—" he squints at his wrist watch "—three-thirty in the morning?"

"I said I was sorry, Pop! Do you want me to say it again? I'm sorry! Okay?! Good night!"

I start up the stairs.

"Holly!"

I dare myself to keep on going.

What's he going to do, shoot me?

But I stop, halfway up the stairs and without turning back to him I say, "Yes, Pop?"

"Who was that out there in my driveway, that you've been sitting with all this time?"

And who was it in here, lying in his bed, thinking the worst of me the whole time?

Holding my temper, but just barely, I grit my teeth and tell him, "Jasper."

"Look at me when I'm talking to you," he says.

I turn and face him.

"Jasper what?" he says.

"Rollins," I tell him,

I study his expression to see if he recognizes the name.

"He live around here?"

He doesn't.

"Yes," I tell him. "Any more questions?"

"Not for now," he says. "But you can tell your Mr. Rollins that I don't want to see his face around here any time soon."

I stifle a giggle.

"You hear me?" he says.

"Yes, Pop."

"Go to bed," he says.

"Yes, Pop. Good night, Pop. Sorry, Pop."

I turn and hurry up the stairs.

THIRTY-EIGHT

"**H**i, rock star!"

That's the way Jasper greets me as I walk through the door. Stretched out on my mattress, with a trace of a smile on his face and a hint of sadness in his eyes, he says, "Hi, rock star!"

I don't know what he's thinking, what he's got to be sad about, but I do know that he's just kidding when he calls me that. So I smile and ask him, "Do you think so?"

"Well," he says, "not that my opinion means anything . . ."

"It does!" I insist.

He shakes his head. "Not when it counts," he says.

He sits up and swings around to face me.

"Not on the night of the Showdown," he says. "Then it's all up to the judges—Arthur and the others, right?"

I can't imagine why he's doing this, why he's being such a tease, but—

"Yes," I tell him.

He shakes his head. "Well . . ."

"Jasper!" I remind him. "This isn't the night of the Showdown! This is tonight! And you're the only person whose opinion means anything to me."

He smiles—that half-sad smile again.

"Well," he says, "maybe so, but—"

"Definitely so!" I insist.

I sit down on the floor opposite him and, looking him

in the eye, I say, "So tell me. What did you think? Wasn't I fabulous?"

He laughs.

"Fabulous," he says.

"And was I hot?" I ask him.

He just grins.

"Come on!" I prompt him. "I was, wasn't I?"

He nods and says, "You was."

"It was just like you said it would be," I tell him. "Once I got out there and let myself feel it, I really felt it! Inside me. Like I wasn't me anymore, but somebody . . ."

"But that was you, Holly!" he says. "That is you. It's just the juicy part of you finally jumping out. And what it does for the rest of you . . ."

He looks into my eyes and shakes his head. "You're beautiful, Holly."

"Jasper!"

"And damned near irresistible."

"Come on!"

"And I'll bet I wasn't the only one who noticed, either," he says. "Am I right? After I left, did the cowboys stampede?"

I laugh.

"Was it 'fabulous'?" he asks me.

"Incredible!" I tell him. "Unbelievable! It was like I was an open bar or something, the way they were lining up to get at me.

"I mean, people who a week ago didn't even know I was alive, suddenly I had them eating out of my hand—like they couldn't live another day, another minute without me!

"Do you know how many people asked, me, 'Where have you been all my life?' "

"No," he says.

"Four!" I tell him.

"No!" he says.

" 'Where have you been all my life? Huh, babe?' "

He laughs at my impersonation of one of the guys who asked me to dance.

"Sounds awful!" he says.

I laugh and tell him the truth. "It was great!" I tell him. "All of it!"

"So," he says, like he's just asking, "did you meet anybody special?"

For a second, thinking back, I can't come up with anybody that I'd call special. Out of all the guys that wanted me, there really wasn't one that I wanted.

I shake my head and tell him, "I wish you'd stuck around for a while."

He shakes his head. "It was your party," he says.

"But I could have used you," I tell him.

"What if I didn't want to be used?" he asks me.

"You know what I mean," I tell him. "Oh!"

"What are you grinning about?"

"I did meet somebody special," I tell him.

He looks at me. "Oh?" he says.

"In a way," I explain.

He smiles. "Tell me," he says.

So I tell him about Jim Sweeney—the whole thing, starting from the beginning, back at Bryan's wedding, right up to the end.

"And just when old Jim thought he'd finally gotten lucky," I tell him. *"Whhht!"*

Jasper grimaces at my gesture.

"What's *whhht?*" he asks.

"Like a razor?"

"Oo," he says, wincing. "Holly!"

"He had it coming," I assure him. "Believe me. I wouldn't have done it if he didn't deserve it! That's not my idea of a good time, busting balls like that, just for the hell of it.

"I mean, just because guys do it all the time, take

advantage of girls, guys like you and—Hey! Now *there's* an idea!''

"Where?" says Jasper.

"Joey Doyle!"

"What?" he says. "Busting his—?"

"No!" I tell him. "Nailing him!"

"Nailing—?"

"Joey Doyle! Yes!" I tell him. "Can you *imagine?* Going to bed with Joey Doyle?"

"No!" he says. "Can you?"

"Yes! I can!" I tell him. "I *have!*"

"You have?"

"Who hasn't?! He's . . . *Joey Doyle!* That's what he's *for!*"

Jumping to my feet, I begin pacing the floor, my brain cooking with the idea, my imagination kicking into overdrive.

"Think about it!" I say. "It's a week from Saturday night at the Cobblestone Inn and there he is—Joey Doyle, sitting at his table with his crooked smile and the fire in his eyes. And there I am—Holly Hanna, up on the stage, performing for him.

"And he's looking at me. And I'm looking at him. And the next thing you know, we've won the Showdown, and the two of us, me and Joey, we're out on the dance floor, dancing.

"And then, before you know it, we're up in his room at the Empire Motel, and it's wham-bam-thank-you-Sam all night long! *Whoa!*

"And afterwards! Come morning, when he's gone, Medi-vacced out of there, after a night of churnin'-burnin' love, here I come, the talk of the town, the girl who nailed Joey Doyle, lazing out the door, looking for more. *Oowhee!*

"Can't you just see me bopping down the—Hey! What's wrong?"

The look on Jasper's face, the way that he's sitting there, just staring at me, I don't know if it's doubt or disapproval, anger or fear, but it's like no look that I've ever seen there before.

He shakes his head and tells me, "I don't know."

"*What* don't you know?" I ask him.

"You're a terrific girl, Holly."

"So . . . ?"

"So," he says, "the idea of your giving yourself to somebody—"

"Whoa!" I tell him. "I'm not talking about 'giving myself' to anybody."

He looks at me like he's confused.

"It isn't 'giving' that I have in mind," I tell him. "It's 'taking' that I'm talking about—like you did with what's-her-name, the girl with the eyes that you can't forget and the name that you can't remember. And how many others?"

He gives me this stare, like he still doesn't get it.

"That's what all us rock stars do, isn't it? Isn't that what we're famous for?" I ask him.

"I guess so," he says.

"You *know* so!" I tell him. "So if I want to nail Joey Doyle, and I don't just do it, but if I take care to take care, then what's wrong with that?"

"It's cold!" he says.

I laugh.

"It's not," I tell him. "It's hot. It's hot and then, it's not. Isn't that the way it goes?"

He doesn't answer. He just shakes his head.

"I thought what we were doing here was trying to cut me in on the action," I remind him. "Wasn't that it?"

"It was," he says.

"But the way you're acting now," I tell him, "it's like you've given me this gun, and now you're telling me that I can't have a license to shoot it, when all around me I see all kinds of guys just bang, bang, banging away whenever they get the urge."

"That's *guys,* Holly."

"Oh!" I say, and I'm really getting pissed, now. "That's *guys!* So what you're telling me is—what? That good times are for boys to take and girls to give?"

"I don't know," he says.

"Because if that's where you're stuck," I tell him, "then I'm sorry, but I've got to tell you, Jasper—you're nothing but another dick, another prehistoric macho man, no different from Joey Doyle and no better than . . . than Jim Sweeney!"

He gives me this look, like—I don't know if it's hate or hurt or what.

But I guess it's supposed to be shattering or earth-shaking or something.

But I'm so mad at him!

"Where are you going?"

He gets to his feet and, as I get to mine, he starts walking across the room, heading for the door.

"We've got a lot of work to do," I remind him. "We need a song, for one thing. For the Showdown. Something that will knock Joey Doyle on his ass and into my lap!"

He reaches the closet and opens the door.

"You want me to win this thing, don't you?"

He swings the door open, wide enough for me to see my image reflected in the mirror on its back.

"You want me to get you out of here, don't you?"

He looks at me, like he's taking a last look, and then he turns to the door, takes a step toward it, and—like *Alice Through the Looking Glass*—he disappears into the mirror.

So it's myself that I wind up talking to and my own image, reflected in the mirror that I see, as—too late—I shout, "Where are you going?"

THIRTY-NINE

It's Monday afternoon and I haven't seen Jasper or heard a peep out of him since Saturday night. I guess he's pissed. I guess I am too. But I'm not going to worry about it. I've got the Showdown to worry about.

"Maybe she forgot," says Mary Ellen.

She's talking about Claudia, who—at this point—is already twenty-five minutes late for today's rehearsal.

"We rehearse every afternoon," I remind her.

"Maybe she got held up," says Stuey.

"Yeah," says Mary Ellen, "by a slow-motion mugger."

Stuey cracks up. "Not that kind of held up," he says.

"Isn't he cute?" Mary Ellen asks me.

"I just wish, if she was going to be late, she would have told somebody about it."

"This is probably her now," says Stuey.

I look at him.

He's looking off into the wings at the far side of the stage.

"Backstage door," he explains. "It squeaks. E sharp over—Arthur!"

"Why not?" says Arthur, walking out onto the bandstand. "I own the joint, don't I?"

"Sure," says Stuey.

"Sure," he says. "And I run the show, too. Which is

why I'm here. Because I've been thinking, especially since you guys won the Playoff.''

"Thinking what?" I ask him.

"That I got a duty," he says. "That everything should be on the up-and-up, with nobody getting any better shot at winning the Showdown than nobody else.

"And this," he says, "you guys rehearsing right here where the Showdown's gonna' be isn't fair to the other bands who aren't and can't, since some of them aren't even in town. You see what I mean?"

"I guess so," I admit. "But—"

"So you gotta' go," he says. "Out." He points toward the door.

"Except for you, Stuey. You got work to do here. Look at the dance floor. Jeez! You'd think we couldn't afford wax!

"Wax it, Stuey. Show your friends out, and then wax the dance floor. I'll come up and look at it when you're done."

He turns to go, but noticing the drums sitting there, abandoned, he turns to me and says, "Where's—uh?"

"What do you care?" I ask him.

"I like to look at her tangerines," he says. And he laughs.

And he glances at mine. And he laughs some more. And then, making a V sign with his fingers, he says, "Peace," and turns and walks away.

FORTY

"**W**here you going with that?" asks Claudia.

I'm giving Stuey a hand, schlepping her drums out the Cobblestone's backstage door, just as she's about to come dragging in.

"Where have you been?" I ask her.

"Hi, Claudia," says Stuey, toting a tom-tom and following me out onto the sidewalk.

"Are you all right?" asks Mary Ellen, carting a case of cymbals and following on Stuey's heels.

"Yes," says Claudia.

But now that I look at her in the bright sunlight, she looks pretty awful in her awfully pretty way, worn and weary like a wilted rose.

"I was with Eddie," she tells me.

"And you're still all right?" I ask her.

"Not funny," she tells me.

"Sorry," I say. "But neither is showing up late for rehearsal."

Without answering me, Claudia turns to Mary Ellen. "What's going on?" she asks her.

"Arthur tossed us out."

"Why?"

"He said it wasn't fair," Stuey tells her.

"Fair?!" she says, like she can't believe it. "Jesus!"

"Mary Ellen's called for her mother to pick us up in her van," I tell her. "We can store your drums up in

Bryan's room until we come up with someplace to rehearse."

Claudia drops her eyes and shakes her head.

"What?" I ask her.

"I'm dropping out," she says.

"What?!"

Looking up, so I can see the tears in her eyes, she says it again. "I gotta drop out of the band," she says.

I don't believe this!

"What are you *talking* about?!"

"I promised Eddie," she says.

"You *what?*" says Stuey.

"It's not his fault," she says. "Terry's been all over him. Asking him whose side *he's* on—"

"Promised him what?" I ask her.

"—whose side *I'm* on," she says.

"What did you promise him?" I ask her again.

"He said I had to choose—the band or him," she tells me. "One or the other."

"Well, screw him then!" I tell her. "Not me! Not us! Not you! We're in the *Showdown,* Claudia!"

"You gotta understand," she says.

"I don't!" I tell her.

"I love Eddie," she says.

"I don't care!" I tell her.

"Because you've never been in love!" she says.

Which hurts because it's true, but . . .

"So what?" I ask her.

"So this is really important to him," she says.

"And it isn't to us?" I ask her. "It isn't to you?"

"It's different for him," says Mary Ellen.

I look at her.

"He wants to do it for a living," she says. "And we're just hacking around."

"Maybe you are," says Stuey. "But I'm not. Maybe I was, at first," he admits. "But now—I don't want to

182

spend my life waxing floors and tuning other people's guitars."

"We've got a deal, Claudia," I remind her.

"You made a deal with all of us," says Stuey, "to go as far as we could."

"I know," she admits.

"And if you back out now," I tell her. "If Eddie *makes* you back out—

"What would you want with a guy who'd make you do a thing like that, anyway?" I ask her. "Who'd treat you like what you want is nothing? Like *you* were nothing?

"You can't let him do that, Claudia. You can't let him treat you like you're nothing. Because, if you do, then sooner or later, that's what you'll be."

She's got her head down again and her eyes on the ground. I know she's crying, but I don't care.

"Even if you love him, Claudia, you've got to love you, too," I tell her. "Or else what's the point?"

She just shakes her head and then after a second, her voice choked with tears, she says, "Okay!"

"You'll stay?"

"Not that it will do you any good, but . . ." she says.

"But . . . ?"

She heaves a major sigh and then, looking up at me, with tears streaming down her face, she nods and says, "I'll stay."

"All right!" Stuey shouts.

Mary Ellen cuts loose with a scream. "Claud-*eee!*"

I look at my best friend, Claudia, and shake my head.

"Bastards!" I say and, bursting into tears, I throw my arms around her.

And standing there on the sidewalk, sobbing in each other's arms, I promise her we'll make the bastards pay.

FORTY-ONE

It's going to be okay. Everything's going to be all right. That's what I keep telling myself.

Yes, it took a little time to find a place to rehearse. People aren't as eager as you'd think to have a rock band rehearsing in their garage. And rehearsing in one of the abandoned buildings downtown only seemed like a good idea until Stuey said, unless we were planning on going acoustic, a rehearsal hall without electricity wouldn't do us much good.

But then, on Wednesday afternoon, Stuey came up with the idea of rehearsing at Falcon Hall which is this building on his side of town where this Ukrainian social club holds its meetings and things.

As soon as he thought of it, he ran right over and checked it out and it turned out to be almost perfect, except for the fact that the custodian, George, wouldn't let us store Claudia's drums there overnight because he didn't want to be responsible if anything should happen to them, which meant that we'd have to schlep them in and out every day and set them up and break them down every time.

But like I told Stuey when he reached me at home Wednesday night, that was a small price to pay for having a place to rehearse.

"If only there was a new song for us to start rehearsing," I told myself.

I didn't mention that little problem to Stuey because that

was my job—to come up with a dynamite song for us to perform at the Showdown, a song so incredibly good that it would carry us through to victory no matter how shaky we might be performing it.

That's the kind of song Jasper said that we would need, back before he walked out the door—or into it—and left me here to write the damned song without him.

But when I walked into rehearsal yesterday, my new song bag was empty. So yesterday's rehearsal turned out to be nothing but a waste of time.

And that's why we didn't rehearse today—so I could sit up here in Bryan's room, stretched out on the floor with my back against the wall, strumming my guitar and sifting through the great wide open, searching for a song from early morning on, for as long as it takes to find one.

And so far, with the time pushing past 1 A.M. and Pop downstairs, tucked in his bed and snoring away to beat the band, what I've come up with is exactly nothing, *nada*, zilch!

But have I let it get me down? Have I taken time out to wonder how I got myself into this mess in the first place? Or if, now that I've gotten myself—and Claudia and Stuey and Mary Ellen—into it, if there's any honorable way to get out of it?

You bet your ass I have!

But has all my questioning led me to doubt that I can do this? That I can come up with the dynamite song that I need to win the Showdown? All by myself? Without any help from anybody? Living or otherwise?

You bet your ass it—!

Wait!

That was interesting.

That chord change.

Dah-dah-dah . . .

Yeah.

That's nice!

Dah-dah-dah . . .

Dah-dah-dah . . .
I like it!
Dah-dah-dah . . .
Dah-dah-dah . . .
Is it mine, though?
Or something that I picked up somewhere?
Dah-dah-dah . . .
Dah-dah-dah . . .
Does it sound familiar because it's good? Or because it's stolen?
Dah-dah-dah . . .
Dah-dah-dah . . .

> *"You never . . .*
> *You never seen . . .*
> *So tough, you never seen nobody tougher."*

Damn! That's what it is!

"I wanna hear 'em screamin' when I play my guitar.
I wanna see the little boys suffer.
I wanna be a rock—
I wanna be a rock—
I wanna be a rock, rock, rock 'n' roll star!
Yeah! Yeah-yeah! Yeah!"

Ha!
I can't help it. As blue as I am, as lousy as I feel, when I think of Jasper, sticking that ending—like a Beatles' ending—on my song, I can't help but smile.
And still smiling, I slowly lift my eyes from my guitar and look across the room to the spot where I first saw Jasper sitting with his back against the wall and his legs propped up in front of him, looking back at me—not like I'm expecting him to be there now or like I'm even hoping that he will be, but just looking to see if, maybe, he is and— He isn't there.

The bastard!

But I don't care, I tell myself. It's going to be okay. Everything's going to . . .

Damn it!

FORTY-TWO

When Mary Ellen pulls her mother's van up to the side of Falcon Hall Monday afternoon, I'm standing at the curb waiting for her. As soon as she brakes to a stop, I slide her side door open and begin hauling Claudia's drums out onto the sidewalk.

We haven't got a lot of time to lose.

"Where's Stuey?" Claudia asks me, as she piles out of the van.

"I thought he'd be with Mary Ellen and you," I tell her as she pitches in with the unloading.

I look over at Mary Ellen, coming around to lend us a hand.

"He's not here?" she asks me, like *"That's odd."*

But what's odd, I think, is the way that she's acting, like there's something that she's not telling me.

But figuring that she'll tell me when she tells me, I just say, "Well, we might as well get started setting up, so at least we'll be ready to roll as soon as he pulls in."

Grabbing hold of one of the drum cases, I lift it and start schlepping it up the walk.

After a second, following a step behind me, a drum case in either hand, Claudia says, "You've got a song?"

"An idea," I tell her. "Enough to start fooling with."

It came to me this morning after I'd spent another long night up in Bryan's room, strumming my guitar and wracking my brain and coming up with nothing. It must have been about two o'clock by the time that I finally gave it up and packed it in and crashed.

But then, sometime around the break of dawn and somewhere between waking and sleeping, I started thinking about—or dreaming about—Aunt Peg and me walking along the beach, the day of Bryan's wedding, and her saying something like, "What your secret heart desires, it draws to it."

And the way that I remembered it—or dreamed it—it was like a scene in a movie because, as we walked along, instead of just us talking and the sound of the ocean smashing against the shore, I could hear music playing.

And it was still there when I woke up—the music or at least a little piece of it. So I rolled off my mattress and, quick, grabbed my guitar and figured out the chords to what I could remember of it—which turned out to be just this one kind of catchy four-bar lick.

Yada-yada-yadadah.
Yada-yada-yadadah . . .

It's not much, I admit. But time is running out. So I'm hoping with help from Claudia and Mary Ellen and Stuey, mostly, who can improvise a symphony out of a three-note riff, that I can use our rehearsals to fill in the rest.

"Has anybody talked to him since last night?" I ask, talking about Stuey and guessing that Mary Ellen has been seeing more of him than she's let on to me and Claudia so far.

We're all set up by now, up on this bare stage at the end of this big empty hall. Claudia's got her drums all set up, and Mary Ellen and I are plugged in and tuned up and ready to go. But there's still no sign of Stuey.

"I guess he isn't coming," says Mary Ellen.

She says it really quietly, like she's talking to herself.

"You guess . . . ?"

"He said he wanted to tell you himself," she says. "But I guess . . ."

"Tell me what?" I ask her. I can feel the prickle of the hair rising on the back of my neck.

"He isn't coming," she says.

I look at her.

"Today," she says, "or ever."

"No!" says Claudia.

"You're kidding me!" I say.

Mary Ellen shakes her head.

"You've got to be!" I insist.

"I'm not," she says.

"I don't believe this!" says Claudia.

"Son of a bitch!" I say. "How could he?"

"It wasn't his idea," says Mary Ellen.

"Great!" says Claudia.

"Whose idea was it?" I ask.

"Terry Kincaid's," says Mary Ellen.

"Terry . . . ?" I don't get it.

"Shit!" says Claudia.

Mary Ellen nods. "Terry asked Stuey to join up with Bent."

"No!" I can't believe it!

Claudia can. "Bastard!" she says.

Mary Ellen nods. "He'll be playing lead guitar," she says.

"What about Jon?" asks Claudia, meaning Jon Rock, who's been Bent's lead guitar and Terry's close close friend since junior high.

"Terry dropped him," Mary Ellen tells her.

"He dropped Jon?!" I'm amazed.

Mary Ellen nods. "He said Stuey could play circles around Jon," she says. "And besides, he doesn't drink or smoke or whatever, so . . ."

"Holy Jesus!" says Claudia.

"But what's in it for Stuey?" I ask.

"Money," says Mary Ellen.

"Terry hasn't got any money," I tell her.

She shrugs.

"He promised Stuey a thousand dollars this week, another thousand dollars after the Showdown, and more down the line," she says. "A lot more, according to what Terry told him."

"If they win the Showdown, you mean?"

"They've already won it," says Claudia.

"We're not the only band that they have to beat," I remind her.

Claudia shakes her head. "We were whipped before we even started," she says.

"No," I tell her, "what I mean is—"

"*Everybody* was," she says.

The way she says it, it isn't like that's just her opinion. "What do you mean?" I ask her.

She heaves a sigh. "It's fixed," she says.

I look at her.

She nods.

"Yeah," she says. "The Playoffs, the Showdown, the whole thing—it's all just to get publicity for Bent when they win—which they already did, back last Christmas when Arthur heard them and signed them up with Peter Karl at ENO Records."

I stand there, staring at Claudia and trying to take in what she's saying. But there's more.

"That's why Joey Doyle's coming here for the Showdown," she says. "So it will be on the news and in all the papers and magazines when Bent wins. To give them a big send-off."

"How do you know all this?" I ask her.

She takes a deep breath and lets it out and then, after a second, she says, "Eddie."

Of course!

"He wasn't supposed to tell anybody," she says. "I'm

190

not sure how many of them know besides Terry. And Arthur, of course.

"But Terry told Eddie that he was afraid, if it ever got out, they'd kill him, kill him or bust him up so bad, he'd wish that they had killed him. He believed them, too—Terry. So did Eddie."

"God!" says Mary Ellen.

"Yeah," says Claudia. "Eddie was so scared of what would happen if it ever got out and they traced it back to him, he made me swear all over again when we broke up that I'd never say a word about it to anybody.

"And I wouldn't have, either," she says. "But this!" She shakes her head.

"I never thought—" she says. "I guess I should have, since there's nothing they won't do—Terry and them. But I never thought that they'd sink so low as to go and steal Stuey away from us this close to the Showdown. Jesus! Who'd believe it?"

I shake my head. It's so outrageous—what Claudia's telling me—even though I know it must be true, I still can't believe that anybody would do such a thing, unless—

"They must have thought we had a chance!" I guess.

Claudia laughs. "How could we?" she says. "With Arthur picking the judges? And him being one of them? And Peter Karl from ENO Records—that Bent's already signed with—being another? And Joey Doyle—who's got to be in on it, too—being a third?"

I don't have an answer for that.

Or for anything else at the moment.

"Maybe they were afraid," says Mary Ellen, "if the crowd—if somehow, we really knocked them out and Bent didn't do so hot, maybe they were afraid if they gave it to Bent, there'd be a big stink about it."

I look at her.

"And this way," she says, "with us out of it . . ."

I've got the answer to that.

I look Mary Ellen in the eye, and I say, "Who said we were out of it?"

FORTY-THREE

"**H**oney!"

Arthur Kilburn greets me at the door to his house—a tired little ranch house—out on the point. He's wearing a yellow silk shirt with a big collar and the top buttons open so you can see his big gold chains and his hairy little chest.

"Holly!" I remind him.

I've got Mary Ellen's van parked in his driveway, and I'm standing on his porch, waiting for him to ask me in.

Like he's as happy to see me as he is surprised, he says, "Holly, honey! Come in! Come in!"

I don't say thank you, or anything. I just brush by him and walk through the little vestibule and into the living room.

"Must be something important, huh, brings you all the way out here?" says Arthur, following me in, and gesturing me to an acre of sectional couch.

I shake my head. "I'm not staying," I tell him.

He shrugs and tells me, "Okay. If you want to stand, I'll have a seat."

He crosses over to the couch, drops down on it, puts his legs up on his coffee table, crosses his ankles, folds his arms across his chest, and says, "So? What can I do for you? Tell me."

I take a deep breath, set my jaw, and looking him square

in the eye I tell him, "You can tell Terry Kincaid that Stuey Ahrens isn't playing in his band."

"Huh?" says Arthur.

"Stuey's playing in my band," I tell him.

"I don't know nothing about—"

"And then," I say, "the next thing you can do for me, you can pick some new judges for the Showdown, honest ones, who'll judge the bands on the performances that they give that night, instead of on some contract that they signed under the table last Christmas!"

"Oh now, honey!" says Arthur, holding up his hand like a cop stopping traffic.

"Don't bother," I tell him. "Because I know all about it."

Shaking his head like I've got it all wrong, he says, "I don't know who—"

"And if you don't do what I'm asking you," I tell him, "I swear to God, everybody all up and down the shore is gonna know about it too, because I'm gonna tell them!"

Still acting dumb, but no longer playing, Arthur says, "Tell them about what?"

"About how you sold out the playoffs," I tell him. "How you cheated everybody that's in them and made suckers out of everybody who ever believed in them! That's what!"

He laughs, just once and mostly to himself, and then he says, "Prove it."

"Huh?" I counter.

Like he isn't just guessing, he says, "You can't prove it, can you? Or you wouldn't be here, would you? You'd have gone running to your daddy, wouldn't you?

"And you know what he would have told you?" he says. "He'd have told you, you go around shooting off that pretty mouth of yours, and somebody's gonna' slap it shut for you."

"If you think you can threaten me—!"

193

"Legal," he says. "I'm talking about libel and slander. You know what they are?"

"Not exactly," I tell him, "but—"

"Well, you keep running your mouth, and you'll find out, believe me," he says. "In spades. Not that anybody'd believe it, anyway, garbage like that.

"Jesus!" he says. "Where'd you pick up this shit from?"

"You mean about Stuey?" I ask him.

"Stuey!" he says. "What do I care about Stuey, who he plays with? He wants to play with a grown-up band that's maybe got a future, instead of with a bunch of girls who got nothing better to do than dress up in short shorts and wiggle their asses in public, who can blame him?

"A kid like him with a juicehead for a father, sits in a bar from morning to night, he's got to watch out for himself.

"But this other crap—cheating people, signing contracts under tables—that's bullshit, pure and simple!"

"Is it, really?" I say, like *"Tell me another one."*

"No," he says. "No, it isn't. It's sour grapes. That's what it is. That's what you get with girls.

"Guys—they win, they lose, it's all part of the game. But girls—if they don't win, right away, somebody must be cheating.

"That's why I always hate dealing with girls," he says. "They're such rotten sports, such lousy losers. That's why I'm glad that you and your band won't be around to stink up the Showdown."

"Don't count on it!" I tell him.

He laughs.

"Oh, come on!" he says. "You don't think you're gonna come up with anybody to replace Stuey Ahrens, do you?"

"Yes, I do," I tell him.

"By Saturday night?" he says. "Somebody as good as Stuey?"

"By tomorrow afternoon," I tell him. "And whoever

194

it is, he'll be good enough that, with the new song that I've written, we'll blow Stuey and Terry and the rest of them off the goddamned bandstand and you and all your big plans sky fucking high!''

He laughs like that's the best one he's heard in years.

"Look at me," he says. "I'm shaking."

I want to kill the son of a bitch, but all I do is tell him, "You watch!"

And then, turning on my heels, I head for the door.

Still laughing, he calls after me, "May the best man win!''

SLAM!

I'm out the door and out of Arthur's driveway and headed back down the road before I repeat to myself the question that Arthur asked me, the million-dollar question—

"You don't think you're gonna come up with anybody to replace Stuey Ahrens, do you?''

It's like one of those hard questions that you're supposed to skip over and come back to when you've finished the rest of the test.

Only I know, if I don't come up with the right answer for this question right now, it's all over, I've failed, and there's no going back.

FORTY-FOUR

"No thanks," I tell Mary Ellen. "I think I'll walk."

It's Thursday evening after rehearsal, and Mary Ellen's offered me a ride home.

"Sure?" she asks me, pausing a moment before she climbs inside her mother's van.

"Yeah," I tell her. "Thanks."

"It's coming along," she says.

"Yeah!" I tell her, like I don't doubt it for a second.

"I think Mike's going to be okay, don't you?" she says.

She's talking about Mike Mann, the guitar player who we settled on to replace Stuey, after spending two nightmarish days auditioning a crop of Van Halen wannabees, a muttly crew of guys and girls whose best licks could sour milk.

"Oh," I say, "yeah!"

"Once he gets comfortable enough to—you know."

"Let go a little?" I guess.

"Yeah," she says. "That's all he needs to do is just to loosen up a little. Don't you think so, Claudia?"

From the back of the van, where she's busy arranging her drums so they won't bounce around too much while they're being ferried around town, and without looking up from what she's doing, Claudia says, "Yeah. I think Mike will be okay."

Which makes three of us—liars all.

"Last chance, Holly," says Mary Ellen, as she opens the van's front door and gets set to climb in behind the wheel.

"Thanks," I tell her, "but I want to think some more about the song."

"It's coming along great," says Mary Ellen, slipping into her seat behind the wheel.

"Really," says Claudia, slipping into the passenger seat, beside her.

"See you tomorrow," I say.

"Good night," they say. "Good night."

As I wave and turn away and start walking around to the beach at the back of Falcon Hall, there's only one question in my mind. Since I know that the Showdown is fixed so that no matter what we do, there's no way that we can win, would it be better to just get it over with and drop out of the Showdown here and now? Or should we wait until Saturday night and let the crowd at the Cobblestone hoot us off the stage?

Because Mike Mann sucks.

And we suck, too.

"And life?" I ask myself, as I hit the beach and see the ocean stretching out before me with its open invitation to put all of my cares behind me once and for all.

I swear, if I hadn't been watching the old movie *It's a Wonderful Life* every Christmas since I was three and I wasn't afraid that some twinkly-eyed angel would show up and try to make me take it back, I'd answer, *"I wish I'd never been born!"*

"You would?"

Oh, shit! Now I've done it! First, it was ghosts and now it's angels!

"Clarence?!"

I spin around, looking for the pesty angel who's been sent to make me take back my wish.

But in the fast-falling darkness, there's nothing to be seen anywhere around or in the flickering light of the bonfire that's blazing just a little way up the—

"Oh, it's you."

That's how I greet the ghost of Jasper Rollins as he steps out of the darkness and into the bonfire's light.

"Hi, rock star," he says, looking no more thrilled to see me than I am to see him.

"Very funny," I tell him and, turning my eyes away from him, I pick up where I left off, walking up the beach toward home.

"Pathetic," he says, as he falls into step beside me. "Utterly pathetic."

I ignore him.

This guy who doesn't even know how to die! He's calling me pathetic!

197

"She says she wants to be a rock 'n' roll star," he says, "but throw a few curveballs at her . . ."

"A few curveballs?" I ask him. "You mean like having the guy who got me into this walk out on me only ten days before the Showdown?"

"I didn't walk out," he says. "I was driven."

"And then having my lead guitar stolen from me only six days before the Showdown?"

"Yes," he says. "And finding out that the Showdown was fixed. Those aren't excuses for—"

"Wait a minute!"

"Yeah . . . ?"

"How do you know about that?" I ask him. "About the Showdown being fixed? Have you been spying on me, all along?"

"No," he says, "as a matter of fact, I haven't."

"Then, how . . . ?"

He takes a deep breath and, like I'm trying his patience, instead of the other way around, he says, "On the night that you won the Playoffs, before I left the Cobblestone and just after you'd been declared the winner, only seconds before your head swelled up to the size of Jupiter, I overheard Arthur chewing Terry out."

"Over at the bar, you mean?"

"That's right," he says. "Terry made a crack."

"About us? The band?"

He shakes his head. "About you. The singer."

"What did he say?" I ask him.

"Do you know what a whoopee cushion is?" he asks me.

"One of those things that you put on people's chairs, so when they sit down on them—?"

He nods. "That's what Terry said you sounded like."

"Funny," I say.

"Eddie thought so," he says. "But Arthur . . ."

"He got pissed," I remember.

"He got furious," he says. "He told Terry the way that

198

the audience was going crazy over you guys was nothing to joke about. And that not taking you seriously was a sure way for Terry to blow a sure thing.''

"A sure thing?" I ask him. "That's what he said?"

"In just those words," he says.

"Wow!" I say, trying to imagine it and finding it all too easy. "And that was it?"

"Yes," he says. "Except for Terry telling Eddie, if he knew what was good for him he'd better get his old lady in line."

"And you knew all this at the time?" I ask him.

"Yes," he says.

"So why didn't you tell me?"

"I tried to," he says, "but you were so wound up about winning contests and busting balls and nailing Joey Doyle . . ."

"And you were all upset thinking that I might want to join your Good Old Boys Club!"

"Anyone would think that you enjoyed my company," he says.

I glance over at him, walking beside me, stare him right in the eye, and tell him, "I wish you'd never died!"

He laughs and tells me, "I'm not too crazy about your company, either."

"Well, then . . ." I say, gesturing him toward the ocean.

"Unfortunately," he continues, "there's no way that I can get rid of you—or that you can get rid of me—unless you win this stupid contest!"

"Oh, God!"

I stop dead in my tracks. "You may be right!"

Horrible thought!

"*May* be?" he asks me.

I start walking again, thinking.

I've got to figure something out!

"When was I ever wrong?" he asks me.

"Some question!" I congratulate him.

"Well . . . ?" he says, like that's a real stumper.

199

"Right from the first," I remind him, "when you told me that you could pull this off!"

He concedes the point. "I overestimated you," he says.

"You . . . ?"

"I thought you had some balls," he says.

"Oh, nice!"

"You know what I mean," he says.

"Yeah," I tell him. "You mean, if you're not a boy, then you don't have what it takes to hang tough. Right?"

"That's not what I said."

"No," I tell him, "but it's what you meant."

He heaves a sigh and shakes his head. "So," he says, "you want to get rid of me?"

"You know it!"

"Get Stuey back," he advises me.

As if I could!

Or would?

"After the rat that he's showed himself to be?" I ask him. "After all the crap that he's put me through? You're telling me that I should go crawling on my hands and knees to that little twerp? That roadie? That I get down on my hands and knees and beg him to come back into the band?"

I shake my head and tell him, "No way!"

He shakes his head and tells me, "You haven't got a prayer without him."

"Neither have you!" I remind him. "According to you. And anyway, even if I could get him back—even though I can't imagine how—the Showdown would still be fixed against us."

"That's a crime!" he says.

"Only if you can prove it," I tell him. "And I can't."

"Maybe your father can help," he says.

I shake my head and promise him, "Never!"

"He's a professional!"

"Never!" I repeat. "Anyway, even if I went to him,

200

and somehow he got the goods on Arthur and whoever, and somehow he got them to play fair—and even if somehow I got Stuey to come back into the band—I still wouldn't have a song for us to sing."

"You haven't got a song?!" He looks at me like, of all the unbelievably impossible things, this is the most of both.

"Not really," I tell him. "Not a complete song. Not a song that's good enough to blow Bent clean off the planet, which is what we'd have to do if we were to have even a prayer, which we don't, so . . ."

I shake my head at the hopelessness of it all.

Jasper heaves a sigh like he's lifting a heavy load and then, like he's doing me this huge favor, he says, "Okay. I'll write you a song."

"No," I tell him. "No, thank you! I don't want your song."

"All right," he says. "If you'd rather have me help you finish yours . . ."

"No," I tell him. "I don't want that either. I don't want your help. Not now. It's too late.

"You walked out on this game and left me here to sink or swim on my own. It's not my fault that you were so dumb you forgot that you'd sink or swim with me. That was the choice you made when you bugged out. So now you'll just have to live with it. I'll finish the damned song myself. Without you."

"Don't be silly," he says, "why would you—?"

"Without you!" I repeat.

"But what about Stu—?"

"Without you!"

"And Arth—?"

"Without you! Without you! Without you!"

I shout it over and over until he says, "All right! All right! But remember, if you screw up, it will haunt you for the rest of your life. I will haunt you for the rest of your life."

Talk about incentive!

For a moment I reconsider.

But then I tell him, "I'll take the chance. Without you."

He nods and says, "God protect me."

I nod and assure him, "She will."

He looks at me like I'm nuts and shakes his head, and as he dematerializes before my eyes, instead of bidding him good-bye, I bid him, "Good riddance!"

FORTY-FIVE

"Pop?"

He's standing at the counter in the kitchen, bent over the morning paper and sipping his coffee.

"Hmm?" he says. He doesn't look up.

"Can I ask you a question?" I ask him.

"Sure you can," he says, tearing his eyes away from the sports pages and looking over at me, standing with my back against the kitchen sink, sipping my orange juice and watching him.

"What is it that you want to know?" he says.

"Well," I begin, "say that you knew somebody who was about to do something wrong."

"Like what?" he says.

"Well . . ."

"Something criminal?" he asks me.

I'm not exactly sure if what Arthur's doing is an actual crime, but when I think that he could be cheating the band that should win the Showdown out of the money that they might win—and cheating the crowd out of the money that they're spending to see a fair contest—I tell Pop, "Yeah. I guess."

"Do you?" he asks me. "Do you know somebody who's about to commit a crime?"

"No," I tell him.

"You're sure?" he says, like all of a sudden I'm a suspect and he's grilling me.

"Yes, I'm sure!" I tell him. "But just say that I did, okay?"

"All right," he says. "But if you did—"

"I don't!"

He searches my eyes for a second, long enough for me to wonder what I was thinking about when I got myself into this.

But then he nods and says, "Go on."

I take a deep breath. "Okay," I say. "Say that you can't actually prove it, but you know for sure that somebody is about to commit a crime. What can you do to stop them?"

As fast as that, like it's no big deal, Pop shrugs and says, "You stop them from committing a crime that you *can* prove."

I look at him.

"Everybody's guilty of something," he says.

"Like what?" I ask him.

RHeeeEEEeeeEEEeeeEEE . . .

FORTY-SIX

*E*EEeeeEEEeeeEEEeee . . .

Its high beams sweeping the underbrush, the white stretch limo with the New York plates pulls off the highway and bumps to a stop at the side of the road across from the ocean.

EEEeeeee . . .

The police car with the flashing red lights pulls off the road and brakes to a stop behind it.

Sssssss . . . The limo driver lowers his window.

"License and registration," says the police officer.

"What's the problem, officer?" says the limo driver.

"When was the last time you cleaned your license plates?" asks the police officer.

The limo driver looks at him. "My . . . ?"

"Out of the car," says the police officer.

"You're not serious!" says the limo driver.

"Do what the man tells you," says a voice from the back of the limo.

The limo driver heaves a sigh. "Yes, sir," he says.

Clk!

"Over here," says the police officer, directing the limo driver toward his police car.

"You know who this is?" asks the limo driver, nodding toward the passenger at the back of his limo.

"Walk," says the police officer.

B'dump!

Moving fast, so I won't have to think about what I'm doing, I step out of the brush at the side of the road.

I hear the crunch of pebbles under my feet, as I step onto the shoulder of the road and reach for the handle on the limo's back door.

Clk!

"Hey!"

He's alone, stretched back in the far corner of the back-seat and staring wide-eyed at me as I step through the door.

"Sorry, Mr. Doyle, but I've got to talk to you."

Sliding onto the backseat, I reach back to close the door behind me.

B'dump!

"If it's just my autograph . . ." he says, smiling like he doesn't want me to think that he's as scared as he is.

"No, Joey," I tell him, talking tough, because I don't want him to think that I'm as scared as I am. "I don't want your stupid autograph. All I want from you is a fair shake."

He looks at me, like he doesn't know what I'm talking about, and, shaking his head, he says, "I don't—"

"Don't bother," I tell him. "I know all about the Showdown. I know it's fixed. I know about you and Peter Karl and Arthur Kilburn fixing it so Bent will win. I know—"

"I don't know what you're talking—"

"—everything! The whole rotten deal," I tell him. "And I just want to tell you, as somebody who grew up in Wildwood like you did, and who has practically worshipped you all my life, like almost every other kid in this town, I can't believe that you'd come back here after all this time and pretend like you're paying us back when all you're doing is ripping us off!"

"Hey! Now, wait a minute, honey!"

"It would be different if you were just some movie star

from someplace else, you know? Then it wouldn't matter so much.

"Even if all the crap that they're always printing in the papers about you being a chaser and a juicer and all that, even if all of it was true, it wouldn't hurt like this does.

"Because you don't expect a lot from strangers. But when it's one of your own! Jesus, Joey, how could you?"

"I didn't!" he says. "I didn't do nothing! I didn't fix nothing! And I don't know nothing about nothing that you're talking about, so—"

"Prove it!"

"Huh?"

"Tomorrow night at the Showdown," I promise him, "I'm gonna see to it that you get a chance to do the right thing."

I reach for the door. "You prove to me that you can," I promise him, "and I'll take it all back, everything I've said and everything I'm thinking."

Clk!

"But you screw me around, Joey, and I swear, I'll curse your name until the day I die."

I step out of the car and into the night.

"And when they plant me in the ground," I promise him, "on my tombstone, I'll have them carve—big, so everyone can see it—Joey Doyle Sucks!"

B'dump!

FORTY-SEVEN

A minute later, after Joey Doyle's white stretch limo has pulled back onto the road, I look over at Pop, sitting behind the wheel of his cruiser, and I say, "Did you give him a ticket?"

He shakes his head.

"I let him off with a warning," he says. "How about you?"

"Me, too," I tell him.

He laughs and, starting up his engine, he says, "So, where do we go from here?"

"The south side," I tell him.

He nods and starts up his engine and throws the cruiser into gear.

RHeeeEEEeeeEEEeeeEEE . . .

FORTY-EIGHT

Five minutes to midnight and all the lights are out at Stuey's house.

"Good!" I think. *"He's probably home."*

I bang on his door and shout his name. "Stuey!"

After a second, he opens his door and peeks out at me. "Holly . . . ?"

I push the door open, and telling him, "I hope you don't mind," I brush past him and walk into his living room.

Spotting an old friend peeking out at me through a crack in the bathroom door, I say, "Hi, Mary Ellen."

Without a word, she pulls the bathroom door shut.

As I tell her, "Sorry," I hear Stuey closing the front door behind me.

Turning to him, I smile, and like butter wouldn't melt in my mouth, I say, "Stuey . . ."

FORTY-NINE

This is it. Labor Day weekend. Saturday night. The night that I've been dreaming of and dreading. The night of the Cobblestone Inn's World Famous Amateur Night Showdown.

With flash bulbs firing and sun guns blazing and video cameras rolling all around the room, Bent is out on the bandstand, blowing their brains out for a jam-packed crowd of fans and boosters of bands from five states—New Jersey, New York, Pennsylvania, Ohio, and Georgia.

Peeking out from the wings backstage, I can see that my crowd has turned out, too. Scattered here and there all around the room I spot a whole gang from Avery's, Alice and Carl, Isaiah and Helen, plus my neighbors the Calderones, who called the cops on us for "disturbing the peace" and the cop that they called, Pop, and Aunt Peggy and Gene, down from New York state, and Claudia's folks and Mary Ellen's folks and Laird and—no sign of Jasper.

Not that it matters. The guy hasn't done diddly for me since the night of the Playoffs—except to show up on the beach one night and offer me his help because he was afraid that I wouldn't make it without him.

Well, we'll see if I make it or not. Only it will be too bad if he isn't here to see it if I do.

I mean, if everything that I've done on my own should work out and I actually, miraculously, wind up winning this thing, then I'm really going to miss seeing the expression on Jasper's face between the moment that I win and the moment when he disappears out of my life forever.

If it turns out that he's right about that. Which I hope that he—

There he is!

Ha! I should have guessed!

Jasper has made himself at home, sitting at the number one table with the judges—Arthur Kilburn, Peter Karl, Walter Scott and Joey Doyle—and sitting next to Joey, the most beautiful girl that I've ever seen in my whole life.

A blonde, of course, who Jasper can't take his eyes off. Of course.

But Joey Doyle—looking at him now—what's really strange is how I have this feeling like I've never seen him before, like the guy that I surprised in the backseat of his limo late last night was somebody else altogether.

Maybe it's because it was so dark in the back of the limo, or because I was so wrapped up in just taking care of business, or because I was so scared and angry that I didn't take the time to really look at him.

But seeing him now, it's easy to see why so many women have made total fools of themselves over him. He's not movie-star handsome maybe, but he's definitely rock-star handsome and—*Oowhee!*—is he hot!

Speaking of which—though I've managed not to up until now—so is Bent.

Hot, I mean.

The reason I'm here, standing where I'm standing, is I wanted to see them in action and hear what kind of reaction they got from the crowd.

So instead of hanging back in the kitchen and waiting to be called into battle when they were done, I snuck out here to take a peek.

And right now, I'm kind of sorry that I did because— like I said—they're really hot, so hot it's hard to believe that any of the bands that went before them could have been any better.

In fact, as I stand here now, watching them huffing and puffing and blowing the house down, working over a tune called "Sizzle" that sounds like yet another tribute to yet another of the "hot ladies" who live and love in Terry Kincaid's *rauncho grande* imagination, I've got to admit that they've never sounded better.

It's Stuey who makes the difference. Watching him now, listening to him as he steps forward and hurls a solo at the stratosphere, there's just no doubt about it.

Just like he made a band out of me and Claudia and Mary Ellen by getting us to fall into place around him, he makes a band out of Terry and the boys by blasting them out of the places they were in.

He's like a master mechanic, Stuey. He tightens what's too loose and loosens what's too tight, and turns whatever he touches into a smooth-running machine.

And now, as Stuey drops back into the pack, Terry grabs the mike and delivers the very last words to his—

> *"Sizzlin' Miss—*
> *Kiss, kiss, kiss.*
> *How do you like that?*
> *How do you like this?"*

And its—

Bleep!

And it's—

Blomp!

And then—*Holy Jesus!*—you should hear the crowd!
Putting their hands together, stamping their feet, whistling, and cheering!

As Arthur rises from his seat and heads for the stage, I
take off for the kitchen with the sound of Bent's ovation
echoing in my ears.

FIFTY

The stage is black.

There's a drum roll, like the kind that introduces somebody saying, "Ladies and gentlemen . . . !"

Except this drum roll introduces this guy, this young
man, who's dressed in a black suit or a tuxedo.

It's hard to tell which, since he's standing with his back
to us and all we can see in the spotlight that finds him is
the back of his head and his shoulders.

And his hat. He's wearing a black felt hat with a rounded
top and a narrow brim, the kind that British gentlemen wear.

In the instant that he appears from out of the darkness—

Ch'donga-dong-dong

A bass guitar erupts in a rocking rhythm.

Ch'donga-dong-dong
Ch'donga-dong-dong
Ch-donga-dong-dong
Ch'dong
Bomp-bomp

A bass drum kicks in.

Ch'donga-dong-bomp
Ch'donga-dong-bomp
Ch-donga-dong-bomp
Ch'dong
Bomp-bomp

Snapping his head sharply left, so that he's looking over his left shoulder, the young man shows us his face. He's handsome and young and his features, like the face on a carved cameo ring, are fine and even.

In the next moment on the next beat of the drum, the circle of light expands until the young man stands full-length before us in his black felt hat, his elegant tuxedo, and his black patent pumps, looking sophisticated and even jaded—like he's been around a little and seen a few things and maybe done a few more.

Joey Doyle smiles. Sitting at the number-one table with his "business associates" and his current "best lady," would-be starlet Donna André, Joey Doyle nods and smiles—as if he recognized the young man in the spotlight, recognized his attitude, recognized his type.

Or maybe he just likes the feel of Donna André's slender fingers on the inside of his thigh.

Or the way that the guys across the table—Arthur and Peter and Walter—can't keep their beady little eyes off her or their envy of him out of their greedy little hearts.

For a moment, and for no good reason, Joey finds himself thinking about the kid last night, the girl who ambushed him in his limo—how she scared the bejesus out of him, how she said the Showdown had been fixed so that Bent would win, how she promised him that she'd give him a chance to prove that he wasn't a part of it.

Well, he tells himself, anybody who'd been listening to the bands that played here tonight could see, plain enough, that there wouldn't be any reason to fix the Showdown.

Even though a couple of the bands were pretty good—Nix, for one—anyone with half a brain and ears to hear with could see that Bent was far and away the cream of the crop, the best of the lot.

And as far as the girl's promising him that she'd give him a chance to prove that he wasn't a part of any fix—"Promises, promises," he tells himself, as he shakes his head and chuckles at the very—

Kidda-ding

From out of nowhere, the sound of a guitar slashes through the air—

Kidda-wah-ah-ah

And joins up with the bass and drum.

> *Kidda-donga-dong-bomp*
> *Ch'donga-dong-bomp*
> *Kidda-donga-dong-wah*
> *Ch'dong*
> *Bomp-bomp*

And suddenly—

> *D'dit-dit-dit*
> *Pow-n-pow*
> *D'dit-dit-dit*
> *Pow-n-pow*
> *D'dit-dit-dit-dit-dit-dit-dit-dit*

Hopping a ride on the drummer's riff and moving fast as smokestack lightning, the kid in the hat spins around, drops to the stage in a split, pops back up to his feet and then, spins around again, rises up onto his toes and strutting like a rooster all across the stage, he sings out—

> *"Your friends warned you,*
> *'Girl, be careful,*
> *He don't set your soul on fire.'*
> *They say I'm bad,*
> *But you know better.*
> *Baby, I'm your heart's desire."*

"Well, now!" says Joey, talking to himself and smiling to his lady, as the crowd breaks out in a flurry of applause and the guys across the table shift uneasily in their chairs.

> *"Baby, baby, baby,*
> *I'm your heart's desire.*
> *Baby, baby, baby,*
> *I'm your heart's desire.*
> *They say I'm bad,*
> *But you know better.*
> *Baby, I'm your heart's desire!"*

Somebody throws a switch and the stage lights up, revealing the band behind the kid, three of them, all dressed in tuxedos, the two girls in cut-offs and the little guy— *Isn't he the same little guy that just finished playing the lead with Bent?*—dragging his cuffs on the floor.

Like back-up singers, the instant the lights come up on them, these three join in with the kid, singing—

> *"Baby, baby, baby,*
> *I'm your heart's desire.*

Baby, baby, baby,
I'm your heart's desire . . ."

And now, with the lead guitar vaulting into a sky-scraping solo, the kid—dressed real dapper, but dancing like a rapper—starts slipping and sliding, jumping and jacking, *One, two, three, four!*, all around the dance floor.

Kidda-donga-dong-wah
Ch'dong
Bomp-bomp

And it's like—the way that he's working—it's like the kid is giving a command performance for Joey Doyle alone.

All his moves—his dancing, his singing, his every glance and gesture—everything is directed at Joey.

But the rest of the crowd, they don't seem to mind at all. In fact—except for the other judges seated at Arthur's table—everybody in the place seems to be enjoying the kid's performance every bit as much as Joey Doyle, who seems to be loving every minute of it.

And now, as the kid comes out of his duck walk, drops onto his back, and kips up onto his feet, the solo guitar drops back into the mix and Joey Doyle joins the crowd, putting their hands together, keeping time with the music and bopping to the beat.

And the kid, riding the tiger, grabs the microphone and—pumping it up, taking it higher, making it hotter, rounding the bend and racing for home, he sings—

"If you can't stop
When something tells you,
'Girl, that boy will make you cry
Or break your heart
And leave you lonely,'
Then, baby, I'm your heart's desire . . ."

215

As the kid swings into the refrain, the crowd comes with him, bopping to the beat and singing along—

> *"Baby, baby, baby,*
> *I'm your heart's desire.*
> *Baby, baby, baby,*
> *I'm your heart's desire.*
> *They say I'm bad,*
> *But you know better.*
> *And, baby, I'm your heart's desire!"*

Except for the drum—

> *Bomp-bomp*

Which continues like a heartbeat—

> *Bomp-bomp*

The music drops out.

> *Bomp-bomp*

The stage goes black—

> *Bomp-bomp*

Except for the spotlight—

> *Bomp-bomp*

Shining on the kid—

> *Bomp-bomp*

As he sings—

FIFTY-ONE

"**L**adies and gentlemen . . ."

Arthur's called them all out now, all the other bands. We're all crowded on the bandstand, waiting for him to get on with it, waiting for him to tell us who's won.

The crowd—still up on its feet—is taking a momentary breather, gathering itself for the big moment.

And here it comes—

"What more do I have to say . . ."

Arthur sweeps his hand out over the crowd and around to the side of the stage and shouts, "Joey Doyle!!!"

And—*Wow!*—you can't believe what the crowd has saved for Joey Doyle. When he strides out onto the bandstand—forget about it!

I mean, it's time for Arthur to call the insurance guy because the crowd just blows the roof clean off the joint!

"Thanks . . . Thanks, guys . . . Thanks . . ."

Taking the microphone from Arthur, Joey accepts the crowd's tribute with typical superstar humility. "Thank you . . . Really . . . Thank you all . . ."

On and on it goes, until finally he says, "So, tell me—what do you think? Are these guys good, or what?!" He gestures to all of us musicians crowded onto the stage behind him, and the crowd responds with another round of applause.

Joey laughs. "Ah, the tension! The tension!" he says. "Okay! Okay! So you want to know who's the best band up here, right?"

"Yes!" the crowd shouts. "Right!"

They want to know.

We want to know.

I need to know.

Joey grins. "Okay! Okay!" he says. "The best band here tonight . . ."

He turns to us.

"And this isn't just my opinion, guys and girls. But in the unanimous opinion of all those people over there, Arthur Kilburn and Peter Karl, Walter Scott, and me—in our unanimous opinion, the best band here tonight is . . ."

He turns back to the audience and shouts, "Holly and the Heartbreakers!"

And there it is!

"All right!"

The kick that I've been missing!

The rush that I was waiting for!

The thrill!

"Oo—wheee!!!"

It comes with the winning, a roaring in the head so loud it overwhelms the roaring of the crowd.

"Rock 'n' roll!!!"

It's over!

We've done it!

We've won!

The victory is ours!

And *mine!*

Mine and—

"We did it!"

And Stuey's.

It's his victory too, because of the way he smiled when I busted in on him and Mary Ellen in the middle of the night and asked him, "Stuey . . . When you told Terry that you'd play with Bent, did you also tell him that you *wouldn't* play with us?"

We hug each other.

"Rock 'n' roll!"

And Mary Ellen.

She's a winner too, because of the way that she made the jump from the nineteenth century straight through to the twenty-first without batting an eye or missing a beat.

We hug.

And they kiss.

"We did it!"

And Claudia, of course, first and forever.

She gets the biggest hug because she's the best and the bravest.

And when Eddie Ballard sidles over to us, shamefaced and asking, "Me too?"—because Claudia's a sap and I love her, we hug him too.

And Jasper.

Where's Jasper!

As I turn to sweep my eyes over the crowd—

"Hi, Daughter!"

"Pop!"

You've got to love his smile!

"Holly—lu!"

Aunt Peg's too!

And Mom's.

"Where did you ever learn to dance like that?" says Pop.

"Up in Bryan's room," I tell him.

"Ah!" he says.

"And your singing!" says Aunt Peg.

"Ah," says Pop, "she gets that from her mother."

"And you, too!" I remind him.

"That's right!" says Pop, looking surprised and breaking into a smile, as if I'd reminded him of something that he himself had forgotten. "Do you remember that?"

I shake my head. "Bryan does," I tell him.

He nods.

"But if you ever get the urge . . ." I tell him.

He grins and shakes his head.

221

"Maybe we could sing something together sometime," I say.

"Ohh . . ." says Aunt Peg, cooing over the idea of the two of us singing together.

"Well," says Pop, doubting that it will ever happen but nonetheless pleased that I'd ask him, "maybe sometime."

And then, wrenching his arms away from his sides, he wraps them around me and gives me a hug that comes as such a surprise and ends so fast I barely have time to hug him back before he's let me go.

"For what it's worth to you," he says, "you've made me proud of you tonight. See you at home."

And with that, he turns and he's gone, off into the crowd.

Touched and tickled too, I look at Aunt Peg, and nodding in the direction of his retreating figure, I say, "My pop."

"You could have done worse," she says. "But who cares about him, anyway. You did it!"

As she takes me in her arms and gives me a proper hug, I tell her, "With a little help from a friend."

She looks at me. "Jasper?"

I nod.

"Is he here?" she asks.

I turn and look over the crowd—a lot of them out on the dance floor and dancing now, a bunch of them crowding around the bar, and another bunch of them headed for the door.

Is that Jasper by the door, waving good-bye to me? Or is it just somebody, who looks like—

The light is so bad up there, and there's such a crush that—

Oh, well! I've lost him, now.

If that was him.

"I've lost him," I tell Aunt Peg.

And suddenly I wonder if I really have—if I've lost him for good?

If now that I've won the Showdown, Jasper's job is done and his life as a ghost is over?

If I'll never see Jasper Rollins again?

"Well," says Aunt Peg, "if he turns up, you tell him I like what he's done for you."

"I will," I tell her.

"Rock 'n' roll," she says.

And she kisses my cheek.

"Rock 'n' roll," I tell her.

And I kiss her cheek and watch her as she turns and moves off.

I turn and sweep my eyes over the crowd—just curious, wondering if maybe I'll spot Jasper among them.

There's Arthur, who's got his hands full, trying to keep Terry off Peter Karl, who's jockeying around behind his table, trying to keep out of Terry's reach.

When he notices me watching, Arthur steals a second from his duties to glare at me.

As I smile my sweetest smile and stick my tongue out at him, I feel a hand, slipping around my waist and, turning around, I suddenly find myself face-to-face with Joey Doyle.

Letting his hand rest there at my waist, shining his coal black eyes into mine, smiling his shy wise-guy smile at me, and talking to me like he's known me all my life, he says, "You sure had me going there, Holly."

Just hearing him speak my name in that voice of his, it's like it makes my name a song.

Sing it again!

"You had me believing," he says.

"Believing that I was a guy, you mean?"

"No," he says, smiling. "That's a mistake I'd never make."

I smile.

Who wouldn't?

"No," he says, "what you had me believing was the part about being my heart's desire."

223

I look at him.

He looks back at me.

Those eyes!

"Would you believe me if I told you that I still believe it? Right here and now?"

"Not in a million years," I tell him.

"I didn't think so," he says.

And he laughs.

And I join him.

And he says, "Want to dance, Holly?"

And I tell him, "Sure, Joey. I'd love to."

And he takes my hand.

And he leads me out onto the dance floor.

FIFTY-TWO

"I wanna be a rock 'n' roll star . . ."

I'm up in Bryan's room.

"I wanna be a major attraction . . ."

I'm playing Bryan's guitar.

"I wanna hear 'em screaming that I'm going too far . . ."

It's a little after two o'clock in the morning.

"When they see me strip for action."

I'm crying—not sobbing or anything, just a nice quiet, totally miserable kind of crying.

"I wanna be a rock 'n' roll star . . ."

"What are you doing here?"

Jasper!

I look up from Bryan's guitar, and there he is—sitting on the floor across from me with his back against the wall and his legs propped up in front of him—just like he was the first time I saw him.

And I can't tell you what I feel—the way my heart leaps at the sight of him, the relief that I feel, just seeing him again. I'm so happy, if I wasn't crying already I'd start now, I swear.

"What are *you* doing here?" I ask him.

I get to my feet, wipe the tears from my eyes, walk across the room, and sit down on the floor beside him with my back against the wall and my legs propped up in front of me.

Jasper smiles that sad-eyed smile of his.

"I asked you first," he says.

"But you were supposed to transcend or something, go to heaven or somewhere, weren't you? When I won?"

"Yeah," he says. "That's what I was supposed to do. And you were supposed to—"

"What did you think?" I ask him. "Of my performance? Not that it matters, but . . ."

He grins. "You were wonderful," he says.

I look at him to see if he's kidding or just being nice, but—

"Really," he insists. "You were better than I ever dreamed you could be. A star in the making. If that's what you want."

I shake my head. "I don't know what I want, any-more," I tell him. "I thought—well, you know what I thought. I thought I wanted what you had. I thought I wanted . . ."

"Joey Doyle?" he says.

I shake my head.

"No?!" he says.

"I couldn't do it," I tell him.

He looks at me—stunned, astonished, and finally, delighted—like somebody who's just walked into an empty room and found a major surprise party waiting for him.

"You couldn't?!" he says.

"It's not funny!" I tell him.

He wipes the smile off his face.

"No. I guess it isn't," he says, "but—how'd you do it?!"

"I didn't 'do it!' "

"Yeah," he says, "but how? I mean, why? Wasn't he—?"

"Willing?" I say. "Yes, he was willing. And ready? Oh, boy!"

"But then . . . ?"

I shrug. "I don't know, exactly," I tell him.

"Approximately is okay," he says.

"He asked me to dance," I tell him. "Well, first, he tried to feed me this line about how I made him believe that I really was his heart's desire."

"Really?" says Jasper.

"Really," I tell him.

"The man's shameless," he says. "And what did you do?"

"I laughed at him."

"Good for you," he says.

"But he laughed, too."

"Hmmm," he says, like a doctor examining a patient. "Good for him."

"Yeah," I say. "That's what I thought—that he had a sense of humor, you know? About himself and everything. I mean, he could have been mad at me for the way that I bushwhacked him out on the highway and practically called him a crook to his face.

"Especially since I either got it wrong, which I don't think I did, or else he made it right, which I think is probably what happened.

"But either way, when I went to apologize to him, he just said something about how, if he had known what he had in the back seat of his limo that night out on the highway, he wouldn't have let me get away so easy."

Jasper nods and says, "Hmm . . ."

"Did I mention that he's gorgeous?" I ask him.

"If you like that type," says Jasper.

"He may not be gorgeous like you," I admit.

Jasper grins.

"But when he looks into your eyes," I tell him, "if you're a girl or a woman, if you're married or single, or even if you've taken religious vows, it doesn't matter! You haven't got a prayer!"

"But . . . ?" says Jasper.

"But then he opens his mouth," I tell him, "and all he wants to do is nail you! I mean, every word out of his mouth, no matter what it's about, that's all it's about!

"Like he told me what a terrific talent I was and what a great song I'd written and how he'd like to learn it and perform it and maybe record it.

" 'Have you met Peter Karl?' "

"He brings me over to his table and introduces me around.

" 'No, I haven't,' " I say. " 'How do you do?' "

" 'And Walter Scott?' "

"The way these guys are looking at me, you can see that they're not exactly dying to meet me.

" 'Hi.' "

" 'And I guess you know Arthur.' "

"But compared to the way they're looking at Joey!

" 'Yes,' " I say.

"I mean, if looks could kill!

" 'And this is Donna André.' "

" 'Congratulations!' " she says.

" 'Nice to meet you,' " I tell her.

" 'Drink?' " Joey asks me.

" 'A beer?' " I ask him.

" 'Sure,' " he says.

"He gets me a beer. He gets me a chair. I sit at his table for a while, mostly just listening and speaking when I'm spoken to.

"And then, he asks me to dance again. Donna doesn't seem to mind, so I tell him, 'Sure.'

"It's a slow dance, this time. And as we're dancing, Joey tells me that he remembers me. Or at least he thinks that he does.

"I look at him, like *'Come on!'* But he tells me that he remembers a little girl, always tagging along after my brother Bryan and his friend Donnie Pelligrino, going to ball games and things.

"And that kind of gets to me. It kind of makes him, for the first time, seem more like a person. Like he's a guy from Wildwood, instead of a rock star from Malibu who's got me on his hit list.

"But then, he pulls me up tight against him, so I can feel him and he can feel me. And he grins down at me and tells me he likes how I've *grown.*"

"You're kidding!" says Jasper.

"So, I *groan,* you know? Out loud? Like a joke? Grown, groan? But Joey doesn't get it. Or if he does . . .

"He just pulls me even closer. And then, we're just standing there like that, in one place, kind of moving to the music, but not going anywhere.

"And I'm getting a little excited, you know? Embarrassed and excited, both. But the thing is, as close as we are—we're touching everywhere, but I'm not *feeling* anything.

"I mean, I don't actually like this guy, you know? Even

though I appreciate what he's done for me and everything, I don't really *like* him. I hardly even *know* him.

"And with all the bullshit that he's been handing me, one line after another, expecting me to believe it, he can't think that much of me, either.

"Except, to be honest, I can't actually ignore what my body's telling me, either.

"So when he says, 'Let's get out of here,' here I am— I don't want to say yes, but I don't want to say no either. So I say, 'What about Donna?'

"And he looks at me with this blank expression on his face and this kind of lost smile, and he says, 'Donna who?'—like he doesn't know anybody by that name. And that's when I think about you."

Jasper nods. "And the girl with the eyes?"

I nod. "And no name," I say. "Yeah.

"But more than that. I also think about how sad it is and how sorry I am that I never got a chance to say good-bye to you.

"And how much I was going to miss you. And how I never got around to saying thank you for believing in me. And for getting me to believe in myself—which I do now, more or less. And which I never would have, if you hadn't come into my life. Thank you, Jasper."

He looks at me, like, I don't know—like he's admiring me or something, like he's never seen me before.

And he nods and says, "You're very welcome."

And for a second, I think he's going to say something more and I hold my breath, waiting for him to say it.

But then, like he's snapping himself out of it, he says, "So what did you do? What did you tell Joey?"

"Oh!" I say, like I have to snap myself out of it, too. "Nothing. I didn't say anything.

"I just looked at him and, after a second, Joey says, 'Well? What do you say?'

"And I just shake my head and tell him, 'I'm sorry, but . . .'

"And you should see him! It's like he can't believe it—that a girl like me could say no to a star like him. It's beyond belief! He says, 'What?!'

"Don't laugh!" I tell Jasper, because he's obviously getting a big kick out of this story. "I know it's funny, in a way. And for all the hearts that Joey's broken, I'm sure he's got it coming to him.

"But when you think about it, it's all that he's got, really—just traveling around and singing songs and making love to strangers. That's his whole life.

"So I tell him, 'Look, there's hundreds of girls here who you wouldn't have to ask twice. None of them as pretty as Donna André,' I point out. 'That's her, over there, at your table,' I tell him."

Jasper laughs.

" 'But I'm sure,' I tell him, 'that most of these girls would be thrilled to be anybody at all that you wanted them to be, for as long as you want them to be it.

" 'I just don't happen to be one of them anymore,' I tell him. 'I'm sorry if I had you believing that I was. I'm kind of new at being who I am, and I'm still not very good at it.' "

"Says who?" Jasper asks me.

I smile and tell him, "Says me."

He just looks in my eyes and shakes his head.

"But anyway," I continue, "I tell him, 'Thanks, anyway,' and I say, 'Good night,' and—here I am."

"Yourself," says Jasper.

"At last," I tell him. "Thanks to you."

He shakes his head and heaves a sigh. "Holly . . ." he says.

"Enough about Holly," I tell him. "What about you not disappearing like you said you would when I won the Showdown?"

He nods. "Turns out I was wrong about that," he says, "along with a few other things. I didn't figure it out, though, until tonight. Talk about your slow learners!

"But the moment that Joey Doyle announced you'd won, I thought, *'All right! I'm gone!'*

"But then, when I saw that I *wasn't*—well, I was pretty surprised and disappointed. But that's when I started thinking about you."

"About me?"

"Yeah," he says, "back on the night that you won the Playoffs."

"And you walked out on me," I add.

"No," he says. "That wasn't the way it was."

"It wasn't?"

"No," he says. "I didn't walk out on you. It was me that I had to get away from—me and the way that you made me see myself for what I was."

I think back to that night and how crazy I was, how horrid, and I try to explain. "I was just—"

"Right," he says. "You were right about me being—"

"Old-fashioned," I suggest.

He shakes his head. "A pig," he says. "A hit-and-run macho man."

"No!"

"I was!" he insists. "And probably, I still am."

I shake my head and tell him, "Maybe you were once, but—"

"But it wasn't what you were saying so much as the way that you were acting," he says.

"Oh, I know," I say, ready to apologize.

"The same way that I do," he says. "Or did. The way I always have. Like nothing matters in life or love but winning.

"That's what I was thinking tonight—that your winning would set me free.

"And that's why, when I first got here, when we first met, I was sure the reason that I was sent here was to turn you into a winner like me."

He laughs at the idea.

"And that's why when you told me all that stuff about

231

my being here to finish up my 'unfinished business,' I thought, *'That can't be right!'*

"But I guess I was wrong about that, too," he says.

I look at my hand, resting on the floor between us, because it feels like—

Jasper's hand is resting on mine.

I look at him.

"You asked me once," he says, "if I'd ever loved anybody, if I'd ever let anybody touch my heart."

"You said you were only twenty-one," I remind him.

He smiles.

"I'd say that was a pretty poor excuse, wouldn't you?"

"No," I tell him. "I'm seventeen and—"

"I would," he says.

I shake my head and tell him, "I don't know."

"I've never loved anybody, Holly."

I almost can't stand it—the sadness in his eyes—when he says that.

"Although I've been loved," he says, "I never have loved. I lived my whole life taking what I couldn't give and hurt a lot of sweet people on the way and just kept moving on, straight ahead."

"And you never felt the sorrow of a love that wasn't meant to be?" I ask him.

He shakes his head and tells me, "Never."

"Or the joy of a love that was returned in kind?"

"No," he says, looking deep into my eyes. "Not until now."

"Not—?"

"You've touched my heart, Holly."

"Jasper . . ."

I can't believe—!

"And broken it, too," he says.

"No . . ."

"I know it can't be," he says. "But it doesn't matter. I love you, Holly."

"Oh . . ."

"I swear to God, Holly, I love you with all my heart."

I've never said it, in all my life, and I thought, sometimes, I never would, but—

"Oh, Jasper! I love you, too. I do. Now and forever, I . . ."

And I kiss him.

And she kisses me.

And I feel his lips on mine—soft and warm and hungry with wanting me.

And I feel her lips on mine—soft and warm and hungry with wanting me.

And I feel my heart break.

And I feel my heart break and so begin mending.

And so begin mending.

And I feel a tickling at the corner of my eye.

And I see a tear at the corner of his eye.

And I feel it edging its way down my cheek.

And I say, "I love you, Jasper!"

And these are the last words that I hear.

And I feel tears welling in my eyes.

And the last thing that I see is the smile on Holly's face—Holly's face—and the tears in Holly's eyes—Holly's eyes—before I . . .

Phhht!

"Jasper!"

I call out his name one last time, knowing that it will echo down through all the years of my life, and who knows what might happen after that.

ATTENTION MUSIC LOVERS!

YOU CAN WIN BIG PRIZES FROM AVON/FLARE AND SIRE RECORDS!

Just fill out an entry blank located in the back of this book; or on the special **STRUT** floor displays at participating retail stores. Or you can use the entry blank below or hand print your name, address, zip code, age and phone number on a post card and mail it to the address below. You must be 17 years of age or under to enter and a resident of the United States.

- Grand Prize (one): Sony CD Player and 25 CDs from Sire Records, including the latest chart-busting album from Betty Boo.

- First Prize (two): 15 CDs or cassettes from Sire Records—winner's choice of format—including Betty Boo's latest.

- Second Prize (three): 10 CDs or cassettes from Sire Records—and Betty Boo, too!

- -

(Please fill out completely)

AVON/FLARE STRUT MUSIC CONTEST!

Name _____

Address _____

City _____ State _____ Zip _____

Age _____

Telephone number (include area code) _____

Send to: AVON/FLARE STRUT MUSIC CONTEST, Avon Books,
1350 Avenue of the Americas, New York, NY 10019.

**All contest entries must be received by June 30, 1992.
SEE BACK FOR COMPLETE CONTEST RULES.**

AVON/FLARE STRUT MUSIC CONTEST
OFFICIAL SWEEPSTAKES RULES

NO PURCHASE NECESSARY. To enter, fill out entry form available at participating retailers during the promotional period; or fill out entry form in the back of STRUT, available at participating retailers during the promotional period; or hand print name, address, zip code, age and phone number on a post card and mail it to:

AVON/FLARE STRUT MUSIC CONTEST, Avon Books,
1350 Avenue of the Americas, New York, NY 10019

Enter as often as you wish. Each entry form must be mailed separately. Entrants must be 17 years of age or under. All entries must be received by June 30, 1992. Photocopies or other mechanical reproductions of completed entries will not be accepted. Avon Books is not responsible for lost, misdirected or late mail.

All winners will be selected at random. All interpretations of the rules and decisions by Avon Books are final. All winners will be selected from among entries received by June 30, 1992. Drawing will be held on or about July 15, 1992. Winner will be notified by telephone or mail. Odds of winning will be determined by the total number of entries received.

The estimated value of the Grand Prize, a Sony CD Player and 25 CDs from Sire Records is $625.00. There are two first prizes and the estimated retail value per first prize of 25 CDs or cassettes is $300.00. There are three second prizes and the estimated retail value per 10 CDs or cassettes is $135.00. Arrangements for the grand prize, the first prize and the second prize fulfillment to be made by Avon Books.

Prizes are nontransferable. Taxes on all prizes awarded will be the sole responsibility of the winners. Avon Books reserves the right to substitute prizes of a value approximately comparable to that exhibited in the promotional campaign, or the cash equivalent to Avon Books' estimated retail value of obtaining the prize, if for any reason Avon Books is unable to furnish the specific items described.

Sweepstakes open to citizens and residents of the United States only, 17 years of age or under, except employees and their families of Avon Books, Sire Records, affiliated companies, subsidiaries, advertising and promotional agencies and participating retailers. Void where prohibited by law.

Each prize winner and/or his/her parent or legal guardian will be required to sign and return an Affidavit of Eligibility and compliance with official rules, within thirty (30) days of notification attempt. Noncompliance within this time period will result in disqualification and an alternate winner will be selected. Grand prize winner may be requested to consent to use of name and likeness for publicity and advertising.

For a list of Sweepstakes winners (available August 15, 1992), send a self-addressed, stamped envelope to:

Avon/Flare Strut Music Contest, Avon Books,
1350 Avenue of the Americas, New York, NY 10019.